LIFESTYLE DISEASES

≈ For ≈

Degree Course in Pharmacy

≈ By ≈

Dr. SURENDRA G. GATTANI
M. Pharm, Ph.D.
Professor & Director
School of Pharmacy,
S.R.T.M. University, Nanded
Maharashtra 431606

Dr. AJAY D. KSHIRSAGAR
M. Pharm, Ph.D.
Assistant Professor
School of Pharmacy,
S.R.T.M. University, Nanded
Maharashtra 431606

NIRALI PRAKASHAN
ADVANCEMENT OF KNOWLEDGE

N1611

Lifestyle Diseases   **ISBN: 978-93-86353-37-5**

First Edition   :   **February 2017**

©   :   **Authors**

Published By :
NIRALI PRAKASHAN
Abhyudaya Pragati, 1312, Shivaji Nagar
Off J.M. Road, PUNE – 411005
Tel - (020) 25512336/37/39, Fax - (020) 25511379
Email : niralipune@pragationline.com

➤ DISTRIBUTION CENTRES

PUNE

Nirali Prakashan : 119, Budhwar Peth, Jogeshwari Mandir Lane, Pune 411002, Maharashtra
Tel : (020) 2445 2044, 66022708, Fax : (020) 2445 1538
Email : bookorder@pragationline.com, niralilocal@pragationline.com

Nirali Prakashan : S. No. 28/27, Dhyari, Near Pari Company, Pune 411041
Tel : (020) 24690204 Fax : (020) 24690316
Email : dhyari@pragationline.com, bookorder@pragationline.com

MUMBAI

Nirali Prakashan : 385, S.V.P. Road, Rasdhara Co-op. Hsg. Society Ltd.,
Girgaum, Mumbai 400004, Maharashtra
Tel : (022) 2385 6339 / 2386 9976, Fax : (022) 2386 9976
Email : niralimumbai@pragationline.com

➤ DISTRIBUTION BRANCHES

JALGAON

Nirali Prakashan : 34, V. V. Golani Market, Navi Peth, Jalgaon 425001,
Maharashtra, Tel : (0257) 222 0395, Mob : 94234 91860

KOLHAPUR

Nirali Prakashan : New Mahadvar Road, Kedar Plaza, 1st Floor Opp. IDBI Bank
Kolhapur 416 012, Maharashtra. Mob : 9850046155

NAGPUR

Pratibha Book Distributors : Above Maratha Mandir, Shop No. 3, First Floor,
Rani Jhanshi Square, Sitabuldi, Nagpur 440012, Maharashtra
Tel : (0712) 254 7129

DELHI

Nirali Prakashan : 4593/21, Basement, Aggarwal Lane 15, Ansari Road, Daryaganj
Near Times of India Building, New Delhi 110002 Mob : 08505972553

BENGALURU

Pragati Book House : House No. 1, Sanjeevappa Lane, Avenue Road Cross,
Opp. Rice Church, Bengaluru – 560002.
Tel : (080) 64513344, 64513355,Mob : 9880582331, 9845021552
Email:bharatsavla@yahoo.com

CHENNAI

Pragati Books : 9/1, Montieth Road, Behind Taas Mahal, Egmore,
Chennai 600008 Tamil Nadu, Tel : (044) 6518 3535,
Mob : 94440 01782 / 98450 21552 / 98805 82331,
Email : bharatsavla@yahoo.com

niralipune@pragationline.com | www.pragationline.com

Also find us on ⓕ www.facebook.com/niralibooks

Acknowledgments...

At this point of time we want to express our appreciation to the numerous individuals who saw us through this book; to every one of the individuals who gave backing, talked things over, read, composed, offered remarks, permitted us to cite their comments and helped with the altering, editing and plan.

We want to thank our publisher to Shri Jigneshbhai Furia, Shri Dineshbhai Furia, Prof. S.B. Gokhale and staff of Nirali Prakashan, Pune for empowering us to distribute this book.

We wish to thank our loving family members Mrs. Gouri Gattani, Master Sanskar, Palak, Mrs. Pradnya Kshirsagar, Master Arnav, Aarya and our parents, who bolstered and supported us notwithstanding all the time it detracted us from them. It was a long and troublesome voyage for them.

We acknowledge the support of students specially Miss Ravina and teachers for constructive criticism, cooperation and appreciation.

Last and not slightest: we ask pardoning of each one of the individuals who have been with us through the span of the years and whose names we have neglected to specify.

February 2017   **AUTHORS**

Preface...

The present book aim to develop basic understanding and management of **Lifestyle Diseases** by adopting Do's or don'ts of lifestyle diseases, in order to develop general counseling approach for lifestyle modification so as to promote healthy living practices. Lifestyle diseases are associated with the manner a person lives. Lifestyle diseases are different from other diseases because these are potentially preventable, and can be lowered with changes in diet, lifestyle and environment. In particular, an unhealthy and irregular life pattern may increase the risk of lifestyle diseases in the later part of life. In today's scenario every member of health care team of health practitioners is witnessing spectacular revolution and transformations in the biomedical science that is inexorably with unparallel access to information. We are stuck by a profound tension between knowledge and wisdom. We earnestly seek both for transmitting our intellectual heritage while sustaining the necessary context of insight and applicability to serve as a required medium of analysis and reason. This is the time to roll out preventive and promotive program with specific strategies to tackle the rising disease burden due to changing life style and eating habits.

Nevertheless, healthy lifestyle modifications are possible with appropriate interventions, which include nutritional counseling, exercise training, and stress management techniques to improve outcomes for patients at risk and those who already have common chronic diseases. Medical studies show that adults with common chronic conditions who participate in comprehensive lifestyle modification programs experience rapid, significant, clinically meaningful and sustainable improvements in psychosocial outcomes.

We endeavor to write in a style that is clear, concise, and enjoyable to read, and to enliven the facts of science with analogies. So the readers from various disciplines of biomedical sciences like Medical, Pharmacy, Nursing, Physiotherapy etc. will develop the insight out of Life Style Diseases in non-pharmacological management and helps to make aware general population about the easy steps to deal with complicated diseases.

February 2017   **AUTHORS**

Contents...

Chapter-1

LIFTSTYLE AND HEALTH

INTRODUCTION

A lifestyle is the pattern of living those we fallow, how we work, what and when we eat, how and when we sleep, which sort of physical activity we do and whether we smoker or drinker. The lifestyle can denote a person's interests, opinions, behaviours, or orientations of an individual, group, or culture. Lifestyles typically reflect an individual's attitudes, way of life, morals and values. Therefore, a lifestyle is a means of building a sense of self and to construct cultural symbols that echo with personal identity. Not all aspects of a lifestyle are voluntary. The lifestyle choices available to the individual can be constrain by surrounding social and technical systems.

We are living in globalise world where good health is of primary importance to adults in our society. This is era of the comprehension "being with positive health" has come out as one of the major concerns. Two other concerns expressed most often were good family life and good self image. The one who did not identify good health as an important concern had no opinion on any social issues. The health varies greatly with income, gender, age, and family origin. Reducing health disparities among adults i.e. over 18 of age humans can be a major health goal. We have some distance to go in accomplishing this goal because health vary widely depending on age, gender, income, and family origin. Self-ratings of health have been shown to be excellent general indicator of health status.

Health: Health is optimal well-being so as to contribute to improve quality of life. It is more than freedom from disease and illness, though free from disease is important to good health. Optimal health includes elevated mental, social, emotional, spiritual, and physical wellness within the limits of one's inheritance and individual abilities.

Healthy days: Individual rating for number of days in a week (or month) considered him or her in good or better than good health.

As per latest report of WHO (World Health Organisation) data published in year 2015, life for expectancy in India for man 66.9 and women 69.9 whereas total life expectancy is 68.3 which gives India a World Life Expectancy ranking of 123. Disease and illness often associated with poor health that limit duration of life and contribute to dysfunctional living. In recent years, health experts have identified wellness as principle constituent for a "quality of life" and "sense of well-being". Many illnesses can be cured and have a short-term effect on health, but the disorder likes diabetes, asthma, stork etc. not curable and can be managed by developing good eating habit, physical activity, and proper medical supervision. It should be well-known that these manageable conditions may be more at risk for other health problems, so appropriate management is a must. For instance, unmanaged diabetes is allied by means of high possibility for heart disease and other health problems.

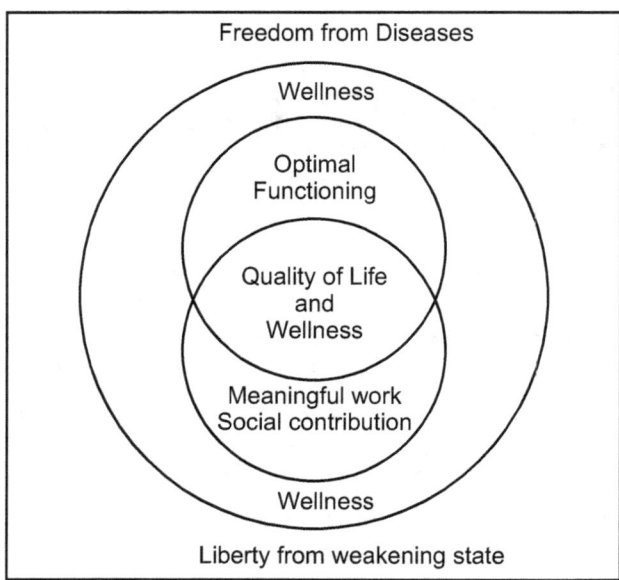

Fig. 1.1: Optimal Health

A disease, illness, death, and debilitating conditions are negative components that detract from optimal health. Death is the eventual opposite of optimal health. Disease, illness, and debilitating conditions obviously detract from optimal health. Wellness has been accepted as the positive element of optimal health as evidenced by a sense of well-being reflected in optimal performance; a good quality of life, meaningful work, and a contribution to society (**Fig. 1.1**). Wellness allows the expansion of one's potential to live and work effectively and to make a significant involvement to society. The dimensions of health and wellness include the emotional (mental), intellectual, physical, social, and spiritual. The Fig. 1.2 illustrates the importance of each dimension to total wellness.

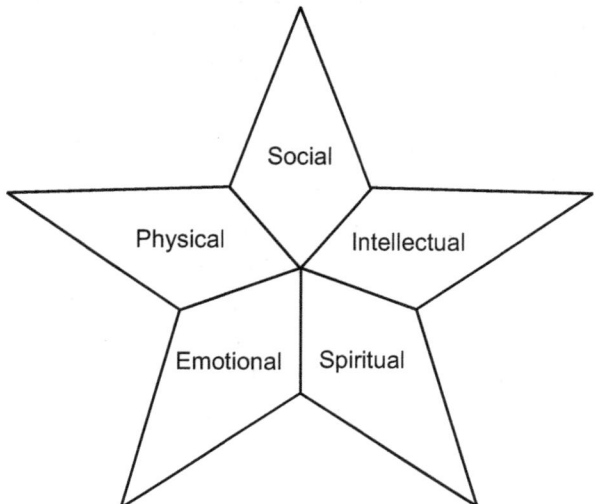

Fig. 1.2: Dimensions of Health

Emotional Health: A person's ability to be free from emotional-mental illnesses or debilitating circumstances for instance clinical depression and possesses emotional wellness. Our goals for health refer to mental rather than emotional health and wellness. Therefore, here mental health and wellness are considered to be the same as emotional health and wellness.

Emotional Wellness: It is the ability of person to cope with daily situation and to deal with personal feelings in an affirmative, optimistic, and constructive style. A person with emotional wellness is generally characterized as happy as opposite to depressed.

Intellectual Health: It is a person free from illnesses that raid the brain and other systems that permit learning. An individual who is healthy by this manner attain intellectual wellness also.

Intellectual Wellness: It is a person's ability to discover and to use information to enhance the value of daily living and optimal functioning. It can be usually characterized as informed, as opposed to ill-mannered.

Physical Health: A person free from illnesses that influence the physiological systems of the body such as the digestive, heart, nervous system, etc. Such person possesses an adequate level of physical fitness as well as wellness.

Physical Wellness: A person's ability to function effectively in meeting the demands of the day's work to use free time effectively. Physical wellness includes good quality physical fitness and the possession of functional motor skills. A person with physical wellness is generally characterized as fit versus out of shape.

Social Health: A person free from illnesses or conditions that severely bound working in society, together with antisocial pathologies.

Social Wellness: It is capacity of a person to effectively co-operate with others and to establish meaningful contacts that improve the quality of living for all people concerned in the interaction. A person with social wellness is generally considered as concerned as opposed to lost.

Spiritual Health: It is the element of health that entirely comprise the wellness dimension; for this reason, spiritual health is measured to be equal with spiritual wellness.

Spiritual Wellness: This is ability to establish a value system and act on the system of ethics, as well as to establish and carry out meaningful and practical lifetime goals. This wellness is often based on a faith in a force greater than the person who helps one contribute to an improved element of life for all people. He is a person generally characterized as satisfied rather than unhappy.

An optimistic total outlook on life is necessary to wellness and each of the wellness dimensions. A "well" person is satisfied with his work, spiritually fulfilled, enjoys leisure time, physically fit, socially involved, and has an encouraging emotional-mental point of view. This person is happy and fulfilled. Many experts consider that an cheering total outlook is a key to Wellness. Researchers use the term *self perceptions* to describe these belief. An individual's self-perceptions in relation to wellness are more important than real ability. For example, a person who has a crucial position may find a smaller amount importance and job fulfilment than another individual with a much less considerable position (Fig. 1.3).

Apparently, one of the important factors for someone who has achieved high-level wellness and a positive life's attitude is the ability to reward him or herself. Some people, however, seem unable to propose themselves compliment for their life's experiences. The improvement of a system that allows anyone to positively recognize the self is important. Of course, the adoption of positive lifestyles that support improved self-perceptions is also important.

In reality, health, and its affirmative component (wellness), is an integrated condition of human being. Each individual is different from all others. Health and its affirmative component depend on each person's individual character. Being compared to specific individual character may produce feelings of inadequacy which detract one's total health and wellness. Everyone of us has personal restrictions and strengths. Focus on strengths and knowledge to accommodate weakness is essential keys to optimal health and wellness.

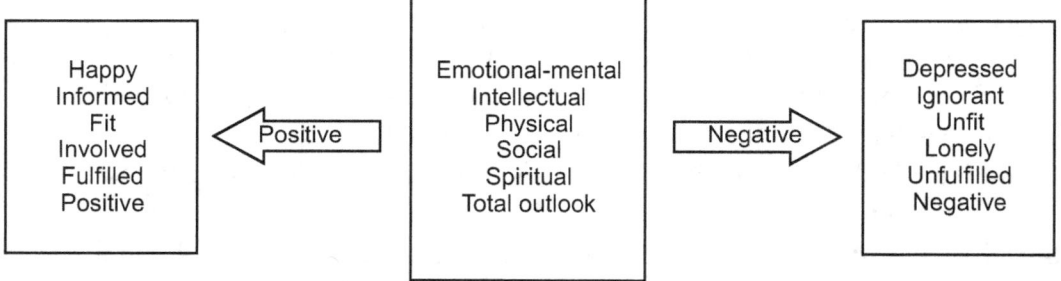

Fig. 1.3: Dimensions of Wellness

It is possible to own wellness while being ill or possessing a debilitating situation. All people can benefit from enhanced wellness. Wellness and an improved quality of life are achievable for each person, despite of disease states. Evidence is accumulating to specify that people with an affirmative outlook are better able to resist the evolution of disease and poor health than those with a negative perspective. Thinking positive thoughts has been associated with better results from various medical treatments and improved results from surgical procedures. Our self-perceptions are vital to wellness, positive view of self are especially vital to the wellness of persons with disease, sickness, along with disability. The concepts of wellness along with optimal health should be measured in light of one's heredity and personal disabilities and disease states.

Physical Fitness: Physical fitness is the body's ability to function economically and effectively. It consists of health-related and skill related physical fitness, which has at least eleven different components, each of which contributes to whole quality of life. It also includes metabolic fitness. Physical fitness is related with a person's capacity to work effectively, enjoy free time, be healthy, resist hypokinetic diseases, and meet emergency situations. It is associated to, but unlike from health, wellness and the sociological, emotional, psychological, and spiritual mechanism of fitness. Although the advance of physical fitness is the result of many things, best possible physical fitness is not achieved without regular exercise.

Hypokinetic Diseases: *Hypo* means "too little," and *kinetic* means "activity". Thus, *hypokinetic* is "too modest activity" with a hypokinetic disease related with lack of physical activity or very little regular exercise (low back pain, heart disease, adult-onset diabetes, and obesity etc.).

FACTS ABOUT PHYSICAL FITNESS

Physical fitness is body's capacity to function reasonably and effectively. This is a state of being consists in at least five health and/or six skill-related, physical fitness components, which contribute to total quality of life. Physical fitness is related with a person's capacity to work efficiently, be healthy, enjoy free time and resist diseases of hypokinetic nature to meet emergency situations. It is related to, but unlike from, health and wellness. Although the escalation of physical fitness is the result of many things, acceptable physical fitness is not achievable without habitual physical activity.

The health associated components of physical fitness which are directly associated with good health's are flexibility, body composition, cardiovascular strength, muscular endurance and strength (see Table 1.1(A). Each health related fitness trait has a direct association to good health and reduced risk of hypokinetic disease.

Table 1.1: Physical fitness terms for health

(A) Health-Related Physical Fitness Terms
Body composition: The absolute proportion of muscle, fat, bone, plus other tissues that encompass the body. A fit human being has a relatively little, but not too low, proportion of body fat (body fatness).
Cardiovascular strength: It is a combine capacity of the heart, blood, blood vessels, and respiratory system to provide fuel and oxygen to muscles and capacity of the muscles to utilize fuel to permit sustained exercise. A fit Person can stick with physical activity for relatively extended periods without too much stress.
Muscular Endurance: The capacity of the muscles to frequently exert themselves. A fit human being can replicate movements for extended period without undue fatigue.
Flexibility: The range of motion available within a joint. It is depending upon muscle length, joint structure, and other factors. A fit person can move the body joints during a full variety of motion in work and in play.
Strength: The capacity of the muscles to exert an outside force or to lift a heavy load. A healthy person can do work or play to facilitate exerting strength, such as lifting or pulling, controlling one's own body weight.

(B) Skill-Related Physical Fitness Terms
Agility: The capacity to rapidly and precisely change the route of movement of entire body in space. Skiing and wrestling are some of the examples of activities that need outstanding agility.
Balance: The upholding of balance while stationary or while moving, cycling, skating, water skiing, performing on the balance beam, working as a riveter on a high-rise building etc. are examples of some activities that necessitate exceptional balance.
Co-ordination: The capability to use the senses with the body parts to execute motor tasks smoothly and accurately. Juggling, batting a baseball, or kicking a ball are few examples of performance which require good co-ordination.
Power: The capacity to transfer energy into force at a rapid rate. Throwing the disc and putting the gunshot are actions that need significant power.
Reaction time: The period gone between stimulation and the commencement of reaction to that stimulation. A racing car driving and starting a dash race require good reaction time.
Speed: The capacity to perform a movement in a small period of time. A runner on a track team or a broad receiver on a football team needs good foot and leg speed.

The health related elements of physical fitness are directly related with good health and five main health-related physical fitness components are muscular endurance, body composition flexibility, cardiovascular strength and strength (see Table 1.1(A). Every health related fitness attribute has a direct relationship to good health and decreased risk of hypokinetic disease.

Possessing a reasonable amount of each component of health-related fitness is necessary to disease prevention and health support, but it is not necessary to have extremely high levels of fitness to achieve health reimbursement. High levels of health-related fitness relate additional to performance than health benefits. For example, reasonable amounts of strength are needed to avoid back and posture trouble, whereas high level of strength give most to enhanced performance in actions such as football and jobs relating heavy lifting. The skill-related components of physical fitness are specifically allied with performance than good quality health. The elements (components) of skill associated physical fitness are balance, agility, power, co-ordination, reaction time, and speed (see Table 1.1(B). They are called skill-related because people own them find it simple to attain high levels of performance in motor skills, for instance those required in aerobics instructions and in particular types of jobs. The sports fitness or motor fitness is occasionally called as skill-related fitness.

There is modest suspicion and also there are other abilities that can be classified as skill-related fitness components. Also, every piece of skill-related fitness is multi-dimensional. For example, co-ordination could be hand-eye co-ordination for instance batting a ball, foot-eye synchronization such as kicking a ball, or any of many other possibilities. The six parts of skill-related fitness acknowledged here are those that are generally related with successful sports and work presentation. Measurements are provided to help the reader understand the nature of tota physical fitness and to assist the reader craft important decisions regarding lifetime physical activity.

A non-performance component of total fitness is metabolic fitness. Research studies confirm that health benefits repeatedly occur even devoid of dramatic improvement in traditional health-related physical fitness measures. Metabolic fitness is a condition of being associated with lesser risk of numerous chronic health troubles, but not essentially related to high performance levels of health-related physical fitness. Examples of non-performance indicators of condensed risk are decreased blood pressure, lowered fat levels within blood, and improved regulation of blood sugar. Moderate physical activity has been revealed to improve metabolic fitness. Traditiona ly wisdom classifies body composition as a health associated physical fitness component, but some believe it to be a part of metabolic fitness because it is a non-performance measure, and it is highly related to nutrition plus physical activity. You will discover how to assess own metabolic fitness in subsequent concepts. Bone integrity is regularly considered to be a non-performance measure of fitness.

Conventional definitions do not comprise bone integrity as a component of physical fitness, but some experts believe that it should be. Resembling metabolic fitness, bone integrity cannot be assessing with performance measures as can most health-associated fitness parts. Regardless of whether it is measured as a division of fitness or a component of health, there is little doubt that strong healthy bones are vital to optimal health and are allied with regular physical activity and sound diet.

Many components of physical fitness are particular in nature, but interrelated and physical fitness is a combination of a number of aspects rather than a single attribute. A fit individual possesses atleast adequate levels of each of the skill-related, health-related, along with metabolic fitness components. People who possess one aspect of physical fitness do not essentially own the other aspects.

Some relationships exist among different fitness characteristics, but each of the components of physical fitness is detached and diverse from the others. For example, people who possess exceptional strength do not inevitably have good cardiovascular strength, and those who have high-quality co-crdination do not essentially possess good flexibility.

High-quality physical fitness is essential too, but it is not the same as physical health and wellness, it contributes directly to the physical component of good quality health and wellness, and indirectly to last four components. Good strength has been shown to be associated with reduced risk of chronic diseases such as coronary heart disease and been revealed to reduce the consequences of several devastating conditions. In addition, good fitness contributes to wellness by serving us to look our best, feel good, and enjoy living. Other physical factors can also manipulate health and wellness. For instance, deserving good physical skills improves quality of life by allowing us to participate in enjoyable activities for instance golf, tennis and bowling etc.

While fitness can assist in performing these actions, habitual training is also essential, an additional example is the ability to battle off viral as well as bacterial infections. Whereas fitness can promote a tough immune system, other physical factors can persuade our vulnerability to these and other conditions.

The optimal health along with wellness can be achieved through good physical fitness and physical wellness. It is also imperative to attempt for good emotional, social, spiritual, and intellectual health and wellness.

Wellness: It is the integration of several diverse components (mental, social, emotional, spiritual and physical) that elaborate one's prospective to live (quality of life) and work efficiently and to make a significant contribution to society. Wellness reflects how someone feels (a sense of well-being) regarding life and one's ability to function efficiently. Wellness, as opposed to illness (a negative), is from time to time described as the positive component of high-quality health.

Quality of Life: A phrase used to express wellness. A human being with quality of life can pleasingly do the actions of life with little or no restriction and can function alone. An individual quality of life requires a pleasurable and supportive society.

Activity Days: A self ranking of the number of days (per week or month) a person feels that he/she can execute usual daily activities fruitfully and in good health.

Illness: Illness is the ill emotion and/or symptoms allied with a disease or state of affairs that disturb homeostasis.

Lifestyles: Lifestyles are patterns of behaviour or ways an individual typically lives.

THE FACTS ABOUT HEALTHY LIFESTYLES

Lifestyle change, added than any former factor, is considered to be the paramount way of preventing illness and premature death within our society. When people in Western society die prior to the age of 65, it is consider being early death. Several factors chip in to early death in Western ethnicity. By far the mainly imperative is unhealthy lifestyles that add to supplementary than one-half of all early deaths. Eleven lifestyles are identified that are healthy and related with condensed disease risk and amplified wellness. As shown in

Fig. 1.3, these lifestyles influence health, wellness, along with physical fitness. The double-headed arrow among health, wellness and physical fitness demonstrate the interaction involving these factors. Physical fitness is essential to health along with wellness expansion, and vice versa. Others factors, which are not very in our command as healthy lifestyles are also affects our health, fitness, and wellness. These factors comprise environmental factors (e.g., pollution, contaminants in the place of work), human biology (inborn conditions), and inadequacies in the healthcare system, to name but a few. The foremost reasons of early death boast shift from infectious diseases to chronic lifestyle related surroundings. Scientific advances and development in medicine and healthcare have spectacularly reduced the incidence of infectious diseases over the past 100 years. For example, newer drugs have noticeably condensed deaths from pneumonia and influenza.

Small pox, a main reason of death less than a century in the past, was globally eradicated in 1977 because of the advent of immunizations. Other examples are the practical abolition of diphtheria and polio in the United States and Canada. As communicable diseases have been eliminated, these illnesses are now replaced by HIV/AIDS, formerly eighth on the list, has dropped since the top ten, not due to smaller number of fresh cases, but because of new treatments that augment length of life along with those who are infected. Many among the top ten are referred to as chronic lifestyle associated conditions because change of lifestyles can be a product of decreased risk for these conditions.

HEALTHY LIFESTYLES ARE IMPORTANT TO WELLNESS.

Just as unhealthy lifestyles are the prime cause of modern-day illness such as heart disease, cancer and diabetes, healthy lifestyles can end in an enhanced feeling of wellness that is crucial to optimal health. In recognizing the magnitude of "years of healthy existence", the Public Health Service too identified what to call a "measures of well-being." Such well-being or wellness essentially linked with social, mental, spiritual and physical performance. Being physically dynamic and eating well are two examples of healthy lifestyles that can advance well-being moreover place in years of quality living.

Normal physical activity, stress management and sound nutrition are considered to be major worry for healthy lifestyles. Three of the healthy lifestyles as shown in Fig. 1.4 are considered to be of main concern. These are habitual physical activity (work out), eating well and managing stress. There are quite a few reasons for stressing concerned about these lifestyles. Firstly, these are behaviours with the aim to affect the life of all persons. Second, they are lifestyles wherein a lot of people can make improvement. Ultimately, modest changes in these behaviours can make remarkable improvements in person and public health.

To be certain, the former healthy lifestyles listed in Fig. 1.4 are important. For instance people that abuse drugs (including alcohol), tobacco or practice unsafe sex can have instant and dramatic health payback by shifting these behaviours. On the other hand, huge segments of the people do not have trouble in these areas. Evidently, these people cannot assistance from lifestyle changes in these areas.

However, the mainstream of the population can benefit from escalating their activity level, eating a improved diet, and managing own stress. For example, figures suggest that humble changes in physical activity patterns and nutrition can avoid more than 200,000 premature deaths annually. Correspondingly, learning to handle stresses that all of us face on a daily ground can result in considerable decrease in more than a few health problems. Stress has a major impact on drug, alcohol, and smoking activities so controlled stress can facilitate individuals diminish or keep away from these behaviours.

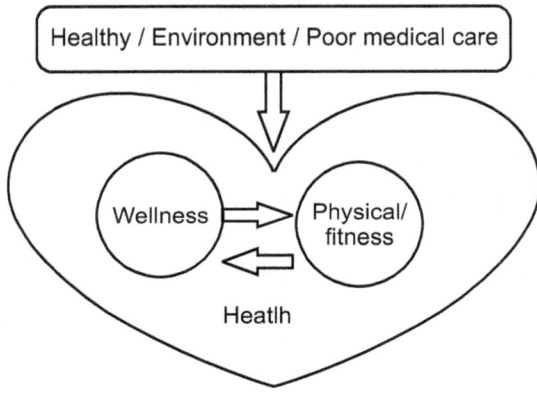

1. Regular physical activity	7. Learning first aid
2. Avoiding destructive habits	8. Adoption of good personal health habits
3. Managing stress	9. Seeking and complying with medical advice
4. Eating well	10. Being an informed consumer
5. Practicing safe	11. Protecting the environment
6. Adopting good safety habits	

Fig. 1.4: Elements of Health, Wellness and Physical Fitness

A lot of healthy lifestyles will be discussed in this book, but the spotlight is on the priority healthy lifestyles since practically all people can attain positive wellness settlement if they accept them. This change in causes of illness and the new emphasis on fitness, wellness, and healthy lifestyles will result in a shift toward avoidance and promotion. Early medicine decisive on treatment of disease, physicians were insufficient and were consulted only when illness occur.

A shift toward anticipation began with advancement in medical science (e.g., immunizations, antibiotics) in addition to the growth of public health concerns (safe water supplies). At present time never before in history, efforts are being complete to promote healthy lifestyles that focused on fitness and wellness. Here, the importance will be on strategies for prevention of chronic diseases and promoting fitness and wellness.

THE HELP IDEA

The HELP idea can offer a source for building healthy lifestyle change possible. The four-letter acronym provides a foundation used for a idea that has help thousands of persons to adopt healthy lifestyles. Each letter in the word *HELP* exemplify an imperative part of the idea. A personal idea that emphasizes

Health can lead to behaviours that promote it: The *H* stands for **"Health".** The theory which has been extensively tested indicates that individuals who believe in payback of healthy lifestyles, are more likely to engage in healthy behaviours. The theory also indicates that the one who declare intentions to put their principles in action are likely to adopt behaviours which lead to health, wellness and fitness.

Everyone can advantage from healthy lifestyles: "The letter *E* stands for **"Everyone".** Considering the truth that anyone can modify lifestyle means *YOU* are incorporated. Nevertheless, many adults believe unproductive in carry out lifestyle changes. Physical action is not immediately for athletes, it is for all citizens. Eating healthy is not just for other individuals, you can do it too. All persons can learn stress management techniques. Healthy lifestyles can be imbibed by every person. As noted earlier in this notion, chief health goals comprise eliminating health disparity along with promoting "Health for everyone."

Healthy behaviours are most effective when practiced for a Lifetime: The **L** letter stands for "Lifetime". Since, the juvenile folks from time to time believe themselves eternal because detrimental effects of unhealthy lifestyles are often not instant. As we grow older, we start to grasp that we are not eternal and that unhealthy lifestyles have collective negative effects. Early starts in life to highlight healthy behaviours in return give long-term health, wellness, and fitness profit. One recent study shows that the as longer healthy lifestyles are being practiced, the greater the beneficial effects observed. This study also confirmed that long word healthy lifestyles can even conquer hereditary inclination to illness and disease.

Healthy lifestyles should be based on Personal needs: The **P** stands for "Personal." No two people are precisely similar. Just as there is no single pill that will heal all illnesses, there is no particular lifestyle prescription for good quality health, wellness, as well as fitness. It is essential for each person to measure individual desires and make lifestyle changes depending on those desires.

Self-assessments of lifestyles help us in determining areas in where we may need changes to endorse optimal health, wellness, as well as fitness. As we study health, wellness, fitness, as well as healthy lifestyles, its wise to make a self-assessment of your current behaviours.

This book allows you to assess your lifestyles or behaviours. It is also important to measure our wellness and fitness at an in the early hours. These near the beginning assessments, will be estimates of the opportunity to do extra wide-ranging self-assessments that will permit you to see how accurate your early estimates were. Remember, wellness is a situation of being inclined by healthy lifestyles. Since other factors for instance heredity, environment, and health care influence wellness. However, over a lifetime, unhealthy lifestyles will catch up with you and have an impact on wellness and fitness.

We can carry out some simple stunts which will decide among the diverse fitness parts. You can use these as a source for estimating your current fitness levels. Later, you will use more perfect tests to obtain a good evaluation of your fitness. Like wellness, fitness is a state of being that is subjective by healthy lifestyles, especially usual physical activity. Young people sometimes have relatively good fitness, particularly skill-related fitness, even despite the fact that they do not undertaking regular activity. Over a lifetime, inactivity seriously influences our fitness.

Chapter 2

LIFESTYLE DISEASES

"If we could give every individual the right amount of nourishment and exercise, not too little and not too much, we would have found the safest way to health."

— Hippocrates

INTRODUCTION

A lifestyle is the pattern of living those we fallow how we work what and when we eat, how and when we sleep, what extent of physical movement we accomplish and whether someone smoke or consume alcohol. The lifestyle can denote the interests, opinions, behaviors, or behavioral belief of an human being, group, or culture. A lifestyle typically reflects a person's attitudes, approach of life, word view. Therefore, lifestyle is a means of building a sense of self and to create cultural signs that echo with personal individuality. Not every aspects of a lifestyle are voluntary. Surrounding social and realistic systems can limit the lifestyle choices available to the individual and the symbols she/he is able to project to others and the self.

The term 'lifestyle diseases' is now commonly used and implies that not only are there a range of diseases that have in regular a behavioral influence in their development, but also that there are behaviors that jointly offer to a 'lifestyle'. Moreover, the use of the term lifestyle implies related rather than discrete behaviors. One of the challenges for this topic is to evaluate the nature of the relationship between lifestyle behaviors and the circumstances for lifestyle change. Lifestyle diseases and lifestyle behaviors are commonly referred to media, government papers and scholarly documents and are intuitively understood by this broad range of audiences. Eventhough there is no consensus about which diseases and consequently which behaviors can come under the umbrella term of lifestyle. As near the beginning of the 1980s, the World Health Organisation (WHO) had recognized the emergence of a concept of lifestyle and offered the following definition:

Lifestyles are patterns of (behavioral) choices from the alternatives that are available to people as per their socio-economic circumstances and the ease with which they are able to choose certain ones over others. (WHO 1986 : 118).

Earlier it was stated that the six major lifestyle diseases are coronary diabetes, colon malignancy, chronic obstructive pulmonary disease, heart disease, stroke, and lung cancer. The rationale for their insertion is that they 'trace mostly to irresponsible living' other authors would widen the group. For instance, Bugel (2003) additionally incorporated cancers in common and osteoporosis as example of lifestyle diseases.

One of the problems with attempting to arrive at a judgment about what comprise a lifestyle disease is the myriad of definitions under which diseases are categorised. For instance, the public agencies uses the umbrella term of cardiovascular diseases (CVD) to refer heart attack, angina, stroke, irregular heart rhythm/ murmur, 'other heart trouble', reported high blood pressure or diabetes. Other publications describe relationship between coronary heart disease, cerebrovascular disease (stroke) and diabetes. It is possible to conclude that cardiovascular diseases as defined by the Department of Health (1999b), several respiratory disorders and a few cancers have a behavioral component to their aetiology and are eligible to be called lifestyle diseases.

Fascinatingly, few authors would include sexually transmitted diseases under the lifestyle range, although they could be argued to be entirely under behavioral control, with none of the genetic constituent that plays a element in etiology of the major lifestyle diseases. Sexually transmitted diseases are more usually defined as infectious diseases, an important distinction for clinicians but perhaps fewer thus for primary care and the public based practitioners with a remit of disease avoidance throughout behavioral change.

In between an 'imprudent lifestyle' and the development of a chronic life-threatening or life-foreshortening condition lie a range of precursors of disease. Elevated cholesterol, high blood pressure and obesity are risk factors for the progression of a number of the aforesaid lifestyle diseases. The distinction between these predecessors, the diseases they predict and the behaviors that are associated with them is often blurred. They are frequently offered as diseases as such and interventions approved by the medical profession. Obesity is frequently referred to using disease parameters. The phrase 'obesity epidemic' is one that has been widely used and characterizes obesity as a disease. Accordingly, obesity can be measured as lifestyle disease by some of the authors whereas others categories it as lifestyle behavior.

LIFESTYLE BEHAVIORS

The behaviors that are usually cited as being involved in the aetiology of lifestyle diseases are deprived diet, cigarette smoking, lack of physical activity and excess drinking. The taking of illegal drugs is also lifestyle behaviour with health consequences. Sexual practices are also often described as health and/or lifestyle behaviors by public health professionals and are considered a key health issue by policy makers. Despite not being straightforwardly allied to what clinicians refer to as lifestyle diseases, sexual practices nevertheless are still considered by the majority public health practitioners to be a feature of lifestyle worthy of both worry and interference. Furthermore, sexual behaviors are a clear source of avoidable and manageable diseases.

Accidents are another key cause of preventable deaths that have a behavioral component, road traffic accidents being the most common. Many individual, local community or national agencies involvement are set in place to avoid them. In contrast to healthy eating, drinking and so on, many of the measures to prevent accidents involve legislation, may be because lots of accidents engage third parties. While citizens may be suggested to eat more fruits and vegetables, they are required by law to wear a seatbelt. Individuals can be disqualified from driving if they are start to be drive dangerously and are forced to take a driving test before getting behind a wheel. Accidents often require medical conduct and can cause disability but do not usually cause the improvement of disease. Consequently, accidents and accident avoidance fall outside of the scope of this book with its focus on chronic disease and willing or act of choosing behaviors.

In consequence, it is argued that health related lifestyles can be defined as behavioral selections made by an individual about eating, smoking tobacco, physical activity, drinking alcohol, and sexual practices.

Lifestyle psychology can then be defined as the study of the antecedents, consequences and interactions of lifestyle behaviors, including eating, drinking alcohol, smoking, taking drugs, physical activity and sexual practices. Altogether a set of conduct or voluntary action that contributes to the aetiology of lifestyle ciseases does not authenticate a subdiscipline of lifestyle psychology.

Bad weather and person driving skills both contribute to road accidents but nobody would argue that such instance related in any way other than their ability to influence accidents. However, it is possible to put together a cohesive argument that lifestyle behaviors share more than their ability to influence a range of chronic diseases.

First, lifestyle behaviors have multiple functions; they are not even primarily health focused. The lifestyle behaviors can be mood enhancing; they can be used as a coping strategy; they are often pleasurable; and they play an important function in the development and maintenance of social relationships. Second, lifestyle behaviors are all under some degree of volitional control, although the amount of control individuals have above their lifestyle options is controversial and likely to vary widely from context to context. Third, lifestyle behaviors are all chronic rather than acute behaviors. Usually individuals will practise regular patterns of these behaviors and their upcoming behavior might be best predicted by the choices they have made in the past. Finally, lifestyle behaviors have the mainstream of their positive penalty in the present and the majority of their negative outcomes in the future. Any lifestyle behavioral change intervention consequently requires individuals to be future orientated. Consequently, it is possible to argue that lifestyle behaviors, although each unique, share a set of common factors that unify them and indicates that familiar theoretical ideology may highlight the aetiology and progression of these behaviors.

MEASURING LIFESTYLE BEHAVIORS

The measurement of lifestyle behaviors is fundamental to study lifestyle behaviors and their consequences and to evaluate interventions aimed at changing behaviour. Consequently, there is a need for effective measurement tools. Measuring any type of behaviour creates a number of challenges for psychologists. Instruments need to be valid, reliable, practical, non-reactive (that is to say they should not alter the behavior they seek to measure) and have the appropriate degree of specificity. Few methods of measurement meet all these requirements. For none of the lifestyle behaviors identified by this text is there a single accepted 'gold standard' measurement tool.

Methods of behavioral assessment can be categorised as observational, self report or physiological. Observational and self-report methods are often not validated effectively, whereas physiological methods are often valid but impractical or unacceptable to the study population. Self-report questionnaires are the most commonly utilised method of assessment particularly in large scale experiments, community or population surveys. Observation or physiological assessments are more common in smaller scale experimental studies and individual assessment, but the utilisation of different methods varies enormously between different behaviors and will be discussed in more depth in individual chapters.

There are a number of self-report methods available to health professionals: interviewing, diaries and recall questionnaires. The choice of method depends on the nature of the problem and the clinical or research perspective. While it is impossible in this text to review all methods available, specific methods employed for assessing behaviour can be adopted in the appropriate disease.

The variation in methods available to measure lifestyle behaviors creates problems in interpreting research and survey data. First, researchers differ in what they choose to measure and second, even if they choose to measure the same aspect of behaviour, they can differ widely in the method they choose to collect their data and the way they choose to present their findings. Throughout the research literature on lifestyle behaviors, different methods of measurement confuse and hinder direct comparisons. On the positive side, consensus achieved by using a range of instruments is more robust than consensus achieved with one tool.

SOCIO-DEMOGRAPHIC INFLUENCES ON HEALTH AND LIFESTYLE

As recognised by the World Health Organisation (1986), lifestyle is more than simply an individual choice. The way we live has economic and cultural dimensions. Indeed the adoption of the term 'lifestyle change' reflects the importance of socio-demographic factors in health behavior change rather better than the term 'health promotion'. Ethnicity, sex, age and socio-economic circumstances and cultural groups all interplay to influence the way we choose to behave. The evidence for socio-demographic influences on lifestyle choices is irrefutable.

GENDER DIFFERENCES IN LIFESTYLE

Both biological sexes and genders are related to health and health outcomes but it is generally accepted that it is gender rather than biological sex that influences lifestyle choices. Indeed, the gender influence on health is primarily mediated through lifestyle choices. Many studies confuse the terms sex and gender. Sex is the biological underpinning, our genetic make-up. Gender, on the other hand, is more socially constructed, it is more concerned with how we think and behave. Hence, when talking about sex we will talk about males and females or man or woman.

Alternatively, when we talk about gender we talk about masculine or feminine. Thus, it is possible to be a 'masculine' female (i.e. a woman that acts in a 'typically' masculine manner) and similarly it would be possible to be a 'feminine' male (i.e. a man that acts in a typically 'feminine' manner).

Obviously, the definition and description of what is typically feminine or masculine is difficult and varies from culture to culture. Few texts or papers acknowledge the delineation between gender and sex effects and actually the terms are used interchangeably. A woman born in 2007 has a life expectancy of 84 years, a man only 77 years (ONS 2007). Men and women also have different morbidity rates. For example, women are less likely to suffer from cardiovascular diseasend more likely to suffer from breast cancer than men (Department of Health 2003). Prostate cancer is a solely male disease as women do not have a prostate gland. Male and female differences in morbidity and mortality are influenced by biological sex and also by gender and gender role casting. The difference in male and female mortality rates is diminishing and this is generally held to be due to changing gender roles in societies rather than to biological sex, although early menarche may play a part in the prevalence of some female hormonally linked cancers.

Unfortunately, not all of these gender adaptations are positive and some of these changes in gender expectations have resulted in women adopting unhealthy, traditionally male lifestyle behaviors. The influence of gender over health is mediated through the lifestyle choices that men and women make. The implications of gender roles for the various lifestyle behaviors will be developed and need to be discussed.

AGE DIFFERENCES IN LIFESTYLE CHOICES

Age is different from every other demographic variable in that the majority of us will experience belonging to all categories of age: infancy, childhood, adolscence, adulthood and old age. Sex and ethnicity are difficult to alter and the majority do not attempt it. Socio-economic circumstances can change for an individual but it is not inevitable nor indeed probable. Nevertheless, despite the fact that presumably we must all hope to become older, older people experience considerable discrimination which has implications for their health and well-being and for their lifestyle choices. There are clear differences in health and health outcomes between different age categories and unlike sex/gender differences a large factor will be physiological changes over the life-span rather than cultural expectations about age related behaviours. Nevertheless, cultural expectations of how people of different ages should behave do play a role both in the way that, for example, teenage mothers approach their pregnancies and older people participate in exercise and sport. Hence, it is important to explore the impact of the cultural influences of age on lifestyle and health.

SOCIO-ECONOMIC DIFFERENCES IN LIFESTYLE CHOICES

Socio-economic is a broad term encompassing many variables and is assessed using a range of different factors: social class, income, work, housing, physical and social environments have all been found to influence our health straight and also obliquely through their influence on lifestyle choices.

This definition is the one used whenever social class is referred to in this text: Segments of the population sharing broadly similar types and levels of resources, with broadly similar styles of livelihood and some shared perception of their collective condition. In essence, different classes have differential power to access material resources: homes, cars, white goods, electronic goods and so on.

Evaluating local environment using the conceptualization connection between health and social class can delineates between local environments by describing them as one of the following: high status, rural/resort, industrial, city, local authority, inner and central for example: London, the relationship between health and social class was stronger in industrial areas than in more favorable areas (high status, rural/resort) suggesting that socio-economic and ecological drawback have a multiplicative effect. However, sex confounds the relationship and the benefits of a favorable local environment were less for women. In other words, the class difference in health was not mitigated by living in a favorable area for women in the way that it was for men.

The women's health may be influenced more by 'class' factors and less by 'environmental' factors. Other authors have proposed different methods of categorizing local environment. For instance the variables are important: deprivation, availability and access, urban form, aesthetics and quality and, finally, supportiveness. One popular way of describing the role of the environment in behavioral choice is to refer to obesogenic environments. The common use of the term obesogenic environment reflects the widening acceptance of the role of factors external to the individual in the development of obesity. Authors now recognise the role of both macroenvironments (e.g. education and health systems, government policy and mainstream societal attitudes and beliefs) and microenvironments (school, workplace, home and neighbourhood).

Less important in this text than attempting explanations for the subtle interplay between various socio-economic, other demographic factors, health and lifestyle choices is the recognition that such subtleties exist. Any one socio-economic or demographic factor's influence over an individual's lifestyle choice can be intensified or mitigated by another. Explanations for behavioral choices are contentious and politically sensitive.

Today our eating practices are diverse from those of a earlier generation in all sense. Fast foods, takeaways and eating out are part of life for young people. There are lots of changes throughout adolescence that can cause changes in eating behavior. It can be very tricky for parents of youth to encourage their kids about the benefits of healthier eating when they are also contending with the influential messages of food promotion and flavor.

TVs, computers and smartphones now occupy every waking hour of public's lives. The expansion of social networking diagonally different media platforms is also changing the nature of social communication. These intense societal changes are most visible among young people. Our new lifestyles have brought about a variety of lifestyle diseases that a majority of urban Indians are facing these days. Problems like chronic backaches, diabetes, depression, hypertension, malnutrition, obesity etc. are affecting both men and women equally. But the point has not come to an end yet. There are a small number of simple daily practices that you can pursue to stay away from such lifestyle diseases and escort a healthy life.

One of the key things you can do to extend not only the number of your years, but also the excellence, is to put together a few uncomplicated changes to your lifestyle. Behaviors such as diet, how much exercise we do, and consuming tobacco, alcohol or drugs fool around a major role in influencing health, well being and the risk of chronic diseases. Accepting what and how enforces these choices, affect health are key challenges to civilization, as are mounting effectual ways to modify the behaviors of diverse social, cultural and economic populations. Lifestyle factors can exert a big consequence on your existing social achievement. They can also have a large impact on the opportunities anyone will practice and widen people's skills departure to the front. The magnitude of these factors changes over your life. When you are younger you have modest power over them, so all you have to do the best you can with offer you are dealt. Therefore, the understanding of lifestyle is essential it impact on the longitivity, youthfulness and personality.

Your fitness regimen of choice says a lot about you. If you treat your body like a temple it will elevate and enhance your personal brand. According to traders and analysts, so greatly so that a term has been coined for the trend in recent years: "wealthy." Lifestyle refers to how you live your life. Your unique lifestyle should be based on your interest, skills and values. Knowing the type of lifestyle that best satisfies your interests, skills and values will help you make a better informed choice. Your friends, your ideas, and your attitude will be influenced by the occupation you choose.

Perhaps, it seems that women are more alert on the whole body because they are more verbal about their approaches. Women will happily sit along for coffee with associates and discuss what they do not like about themselves, whereas men alternatively, do not let their sentinel down as much just about their buddy. This possibly since they have to uphold their manly we 'love beer, football, and girls' loom to life. The celebrities indisputably plays a part in making both men and women body conscious. Seeing the celebrity on our TV screens is enough to make anyone want to be them, or be with them. With more and more girls lusting following these celebrity hunks, and vice-versa, it is logical that the world is becoming more self cognizant. However, let's not forget the widespread teams these people have to help them look that stunning, and the money they have to put behind it. Moreover, your ideal indicates your lifestyle. Therefore, the people attract toward them and follow their style and considered as a status symbol.

Lifestyle diseases are spreading very rapidly in every corner of all countries. These are different from other diseases because they are potentially avoidable, and can be prohibited with the changes in diet and everyday life.

More interestingly, a healthy or unhealthy lifestyle will most likely be carry forwarded across inheritance. As per the study when a 0-3 years old child has a mother who habituates of a healthy lifestyle, this kid will be 27% more likely to turn into healthy and adopt the same lifestyle. For instance, high earnings parents are more prone to eat natural food, have time to work out, and provide the best living situation to children. In contrast, low earnings parents are more liable to take part in unhealthy actions such as smoking to assist those releases poverty-related stress and despair. Parents are the first teacher for every child. The whole thing that parents do will be very expected to be transferred to their kids through the learning process.

Modern science through better cleanliness, immunization and antibiotics, and medical attention has eliminated the danger of death from most contagious diseases. It means that death from lifestyle diseases like heart disease and cancer are now the key reasons of death. Everyone as expected has to die of something, but lifestyle diseases take people prior to their moment in time. A lot of citizens are dying fairly young from Heart Disease and Cancer and other lifestyle diseases in contemporary times.

As on date in India, the circumstances are to a certain extent alarming. The disease outline is shifting quickly. The WHO has recognized India as one of the nations that is going to have most of the lifestyle diseases in close proximity to future. At the present time, not only are lifestyle diseases becoming more frequent, but they are also touching younger people. Hence, the population at risk shifts from 40+ to may be 30+ or even younger. Already measured the diabetes capital of the world, India at this instant appears headed towards gaining an additional dubious peculiarity of becoming the lifestyle-related disease capital too. As per the report published jointly by the All India Institute of Medical Sciences and Max Hospital shows the frequency of hypertension, obesity and heart disease is escalating at an alarming rate, particularly in the young, metropolitan population. As per doctors say, a sedentary lifestyle collective with an increase in the utilization of fatty food and alcohol is to blame cases of obesity, diabetes, hypertension etc.

Most of the lifestyle diseases, for example : diabetes or heart disease, influence the individual in the productive years. They are responsible for the condensed productivity and before time departure. Furthermore, they put enormous pressure on public health expenses as in most cases the treatment expenses are higher in comparison to communicable diseases.

Dietary salt restriction is well known to reduce blood pressure and pre-hypertensives should be pessimistic to lower their dietary salt use. Therefore, limitations on food products to promote the population to accept healthy dietary practices are unwanted in the Indian context, contrasting to the developed nations. Campaigns through the audio-visual media, newspapers and health magazine might be functonal strategies in the country.

Nevertheless, healthy lifestyle modifications are possible with suitable interventions, which include nutritional psychoanalysis, exercise instruction and stress executing techniques to develop outcomes for patients at risk and those who by now have general chronic diseases. Medical studies illustrate those adults with universal chronic conditions who participate in broad lifestyle modification programs experience rapid, significant, clinically important and sustainable improvements in laboratory and psychosocial outcomes.

Chapter 3

DIABETES MELLITUS

Think about it: Heart disease and diabetes, which account for more deaths in the worldwide than everything else combined, are completely preventable by making comprehensive lifestyle change, without drugs or surgery.

— *Dean Ornish*

INTRODUCTION

Diabetes is chief public health trouble globally with an ever-increasing disease trend. A sum of 366 million (8.3%) citizens lived with diabetes in 2011 and 4.6 million deaths were credited to diabetes. The frequency is estimated to amplify to double the 2011 data to 552 million in 2030 (International Diabetes Federation n.d.), if no deed is taken. The diabetes pandemic is worse in developing Asian countries. Asian nations are at significant risk of diabetes in relationship to western societies, because of their altering life style.

Diabetes mellitus type 2 (in earlier times Non-Insulin Dependent Diabetes Mellitus (NIDDM) or else adult-onset diabetes) is a metabolic disorder that is characterized by hyperglycemia (high blood sugar) in the context of insulin resistance and relative lack of insulin. Rates of type 2 diabetes have increased markedly since 1960 in parallel with obesity. As of 2010 there were roughly 285 million citizens diagnosed by the disease compared to approximately 30 million in 1985. Type 2 diabetes is classically a chronic disease related with a ten year shorter life expectancy.

The classic symptoms are excess thirst, frequent urination, and constant hunger. Long-term complications from high blood sugar can include diabetic retinopathy where eyesight is affected, heart disease, strokes, kidney breakdown which may necessitate dialysis, and poor blood flow in the limbs leading to amputations. The acute complication of ketoacidosis, a feature of type 1 diabetes, is uncommon; however hyperosmolar hyperglycemic condition may takes place.

The increase in diabetes population thought to be primarily because of the global population aging, a decline in work out, and increasing rates of obesity. The five countries with the greatest number of natives with diabetes on or after 2000 are India having (31.7), China (20.8), the United States (17.7), Indonesia (8.4), and Japan (6.8) millions. Hence, now it is recognized as a global outbreak by the World Health Organization.

COMMON MYTH AND MISUNDERSTANDINGS

There are a lot of myths regarding diabetes that make it tricky for people to consider some of the solid facts such as diabetes are a serious and potentially lethal disease. The following myths and misunderstandings are pragmatic in day to day life.

- Diabetes is not that severe problem.
- People with diabetes should consume special diabetic foods.
- If you diabetic, you eat small amounts of starchy foods, such as bread, potatoes along with pasta.
- Diabetics can not eat sweets or chocolate
- Fruit is a healthy food, hence it is ok to eat as much as you want.
- Eating too much sweet food that causes diabetes.
- Young people would not have diabetes.
- Patients only need to take medicines when they have diabetes.
- Dietary treatment is to control the intake of sugar and staple food.
- The lower blood sugar is the better.
- Eating more hypoglycemic drugs can avoid the diet control.
- The monitor of diabetes only needs to monitor blood sugar.

CAUSES

The progress of type 2 diabetes is causes due to a combination of genetic factors as well as lifestyle. While some of these factors are under personal control, such as diet and obesity as compared to other factors, for instance increasing age, genetics in addition to female gender. A deficient sleep has been related to type 2 diabetes; it is believed to act through its effect on metabolism. The dietary condition of a mother throughout fetal development may as well play a role, with one anticipated mechanism of being altered DNA methylation. It is caused by insulin resistance in the liver and skeletal muscle, amplified glucose production in the liver, over production of free fatty acids via fat cells and relation insulin shortage.

- Insulin secretion decline with gradual beta cell failure.
- Reduced blood glucose levels often can be achieved via alteration in food intake and physical activity patterns. Oral medication and insulin supplementation are in time required.
- Contributing factors are obesity, Age (commencement of puberty is related with augmented insulin resistance), lack of physical activity, genetic predisposition, racial/ethnic background (Asian/Pacific Islander Native American, African and American Hispanic).
- Conditions related with insulin resistance, (e.g., polycystic ovary syndrome)

The recommendations of American Diabetes Association for testing to detect pre-diabetes and type-2 diabetes are considered in adults devoid of symptoms. The people, who are with or without risk factors, should begin testing at age 45. Risk factors for pre-diabetes and diabetes is adding to being overweight or being age 45 or senior comprises the following:

- Person who is physically inactive.
- Having a parent, brother, or sister with diabetes.
- Having a family background.
- Giving birth to a baby weighing more than 9 pounds or being diagnosed with gestational diabetic, diabetes first institute in pregnancy.
- Having towering blood pressure 140/90 mmHg or above or being treated for high blood pressure.
- Having HDL, below 35 mg/dL, or a triglyceride above 250 mg/dL.
- Possessing Polycystic Ovary Syndrome (PCOS).
- Having Impaired Glucose Tolerance (IGT) or Fasting Glucose (IFG) on previous testing.
- Having other circumstances associated with insulin resistance, for instance severe obesity.
- Having a history of cardiovascular disease.

If results of testing are normal, testing should be repetitive at least every 3 years. Doctors may advocate more frequent testing depending on initial results and risk status.

COMPLICATIONS

Type 2 diabetes is typically a chronic disease coupled with a ten-year shorter living expectancy. This is partially due to a numeral of complications through which it is attached, including: two to four times the risk of cardiovascular disease, together with ischemic heart disease and stroke; a 20-fold enhancement in lower limb amputations, and increased rates of hospitalizations. In the developed world, and increasingly elsewhere, type 2 diabetes is the prevalent source of non-traumatic blindness along with kidney failure. It has also been allied with an improved possibility of cognitive dysfunction and dementia throughout disease processes for instance Alzheimer's disease and vascular dementia. Further complications embrace acanthosis nigricans, sexual dysfunction, and frequent infections, nerve damage (neuropathy), foot damage, skin conditions and hearing impairment.

MANAGEMENT

Management of type 2 diabetes focuses on lifestyle interventions, lowering other cardiovascular risk factors, and maintaining blood glucose levels in the usual range. Own-monitoring of blood glucose with newly diagnosed type 2 diabetes perhaps used in combination with education. However the benefit of self monitoring in individuals not using multi-dose insulin is disputed. In persons who do not desire to measure blood levels, measuring urine levels may be done. Managing other cardiovascular risk factors, for example, hypertension, high cholesterol, and microalbuminuria, increases an individual's life expectancy. Decreasing the systolic blood pressure to less than 140 mmHg is associated with a lower risk of death and improved outcomes. Thorough blood pressure (less than 130/80 mmHg) management as contrasting to standard blood pressure management (less than 140/85–100 mmHg) results in a slight decline in stroke risk but no effect on overall risk of death.

MEDICATION

There are quite a few classes of anti-diabetic medications on hand. Metformin is generally suggested a first line treatment since it decreases mortality. But it should not be used in persons with kidney or liver problems. Other drug from another class or insulin may be added if metformin is not sufficient after three months. Further, classes of medications include: sulfonylureas, dipeptidyl peptidase-4 inhibitors thiazolidinediones, etc. Rosiglitazone, a thiazolidinedione, has not been found to improve long-term outcomes even though it improves blood sugar levels. Moreover it is coupled with increased rates of heart disease as well as death also. Angiotensin converting enzyme inhibitors prevent kidney disease and improve outcomes in those with diabetes. The similar medications angiotensin receptor blockers do not.

Injections of insulin possibly added to oral medication or used alone. Most people do not initially need insulin. When it is used, a long-acting formulation is typically added at night, with oral medications being continued. When nightly insulin is insufficient, twice daily insulin may achieve better control.

IMPORTANCE OF LIFESTYLE

Qualities of Life (QoL) vary with persons, societies, community with diabetes and non-diabetes. It depends on diet and physical activity, scheming the disease complications and health improvements gifted. Quality of life is known to affect mental, physical, social well-being and daily lives. The prevalence of depression is higher in diabetic than non-diabetic persons with significant differences in quality of life indices between depression with diabetes and non-diabetes. Psychological distresses (depression, anxiety and sleep disturbances) can boast a harmful impact on QoL. The threat of depression is elevated in diabetes, undiagnosed diabetes and impaired glucose metabolism that have serious threat to QoL. In addition, peripheral neuropathy as well as retinopathy, kidney disease, and coronary disease like complications affects fitness related QoL in diabetic. Thus, it should be higher priority in prevention and control of diabetes.

Evidence has exposed that effective anticipatory program can help in decreasing or delaying the occurrence of diabetes and pre-diabetes and improves QoL. Age, sex, education, smoking, alcohol use, occupation, income, history of cardiovascular disease, physical activity, a large body mass index and waist circumference are connected with impaired fasting glucose and diabetes. It is known that diabetes can be prevented by modification to a healthy among high risk groups.

LIFE STYLE MODIFICATIONS

The life style of individual is focusing on their diet, weight, physical activity, tobacco smoking and alcohol drinking, has notorious that out of which factors weight loss is the main predictor in the anticipation of diabetes. There are many effective means in the reduction of weight loss e.g. low fat and calorie diets, high fibre or protein rich diets coupled with regular exercise. Individualized dietary counseling, course type resistance training sitting and guidance on escalating physical activity reduces the weight and risks of diabetes. A person with diabetes, achieving reasonable weight loss with physical activity possibly will control his blood sugar and improve insulin sensitivity. A small group weight loss session is important in prevention of diabetes. A randomized control trial found noteworthy weight loss in both hypo-caloric almond-enriched diet and nut-free diet groups but comparatively smaller scale of weight loss in hypo-caloric almond-enriched diet.

Life style modification reduces diabetes incidence up to 55%, and delays disease progression as well as managing diabetes symptoms successfully. Lifestyle intervention (diet and exercise) can reduce the rate of diabetes by 28-59% within impaired fasting glucose and/or impaired glucose tolerance. A community based life style prevention measure reduced the fasting blood sugar level of diabetes and pre-diabetes by 25% and 11% respectively. The lifestyle interventions are identified as more effective than anti-diabetic medicines.

It has been reported that efficient lifestyle programs prevent diabetes by 58% while Metformin only by 31% (Diabetes Prevention Program Research Group, 2002). Therefore, lifestyle change activity can be more effective, cheaper and safer than anti-diabetic medications. Lifestyle intervention is feasible in primary health care settings with a higher level of education. It significantly reduces the weight, waist measurements, lipid analysis glucose levels, and psychological distress.

However, it is not always easy to replicate lifestyle intervention programs in developing countries even in sound funded health care systems, as it need a co-ordinated attempt among government, society and funding sources. Behaviour change to modify lifestyle is another challenge in the anticipation of diabetes as it requires substantial effort, motivation and time.

The counseling can be useful motive for people in changing their behaviour internally. A short term goal setting and problem solving techniques with social support and regular follow-up programs are helpful to uphold life style behaviour alteration. The deliverance of group exercise by peers is more valuable than the availability of guidelines to manage obesity and cardio-metabolic risk factors. Modification of dietary behaviour, physical activity and smoking behaviour can be sustained by combination of two counseling methods e.g. motivational interviewing and problem solving treatment.

DIETARY THERAPY

The dietary factors influence the risk of developing type 2 diabetes. Utilization of sugar-sweetened drinks in excess is coupled with a greater than before risk. The type of fats within the diet is as well important, with saturated fats and Trans fatty acids increasing the risk. Whereas, polyunsaturated and monounsaturated fat decreasing the risk. A consumption lot of white rice appears to play a role in increasing risk. Persistent organic pollutants may also play a role.

An appropriate diet and exercise are the fundamentals of diabetic care, with a greater quantity of exercise yielding enhanced results. Aerobic workout leads to a decline in HbA1c and improved insulin sensitivity. Resistance guidance is also useful and the amalgamation of both types of exercise perhaps most effective. A diabetic diet to facilitate weight loss is important. At the same time what is the best diet type to achieve this is controversial, a low glycemic index diet or low carbohydrate diet has been found to improve blood sugar control. Culturally suitable education may help people with type 2 diabetes control their blood sugar levels, for up to six months at least. If changes in lifestyle in those with mild diabetes have not resulted in improved blood sugars within six weeks, medications should then be considered. There is not sufficient evidence to determine if lifestyle interventions affect mortality in those who already have type 2 diabetes.

Many policy makers are looking thoughtfully to introduce a tax on unhealthy foods. For example, Denmark introduces the 'fat tax' for high saturated fat (more than 2.3%) foods: butter, milk, cheese, pizza, meat, oil and processed foods. Some scientists suggest that salt, sugar and refined carbohydrate should be treated the same as fat, as these are more harmful to health. Hungary and France have introduced a junk food tax with sweetened drinks at the same time as Peru has considered implementing a similar tax. Furthermore, there is no connection between reducing sugar intake and reducing the incidence of obesity. Recently, in India also as media report the selling of junk food are banned in educational campus.

PHYSICAL ACTIVITY

Usual physical activity increases the functions of the body and reduces the danger of diabetes (Harvard School of Public Health, 2012). Well-structured physical activity is valuable in reducing the prevalence of diabetes and restoring normal glucose events among high risk groups. An inactive physical lifestyle may boost diabetes and impaired fasting glucose with low down treadmill exercise related to rise of diabetes impaired fasting glucose. Lack of physical activity excluding walking is a risk of diabetes. A challenge exists in developing, implementing and evaluating efficient low cost prevention programs at the local level. A single program for people with newly diagnosed diabetes does not make a distinction in biomedical changes plus lifestyle outcomes over a year's period. Although a sign of improvement in some health beliefs to develop helpful diabetes teaching agenda is ethnically relevant in a developing country background is required.

Intervention is more effective with social support, follow-up, using self–setting behaviour change and self-monitoring. Diet and exercise is the most important device of life; dropping weight, eating the right food and habitual exercise are central to the management of diabetes rather than medical treatment. Choosing healthy food is important, as is overriding suitable food on a estimated basis. These foods can decrease weight and blood glucose but most importantly they assist in reducing the risk of heart disease and high cholesterol.

PREVENTION

Type 1 Diabetes:

Presently, there is no way to prevent type 1 diabetes. Current research with relatives of people with type 1 diabetes is studying how to prevent or delay the autoimmune destruction of the beta cells. If a simple blood test detects the presence of islet cell antibodies, the person is eligible to enter.

Type 2 Diabetes:

Prevention requires identifying those children and teens at risk and providing them appropriate knowledge, resources, and support to help to reduce risk factors.

- Since 40-80% of teens diagnosed with type 2 diabetic are overweight and the incidence of overweight is increasing, primary prevention of type 2 diabetes in young person should include a health approach that targets the general population. Health professionals need to be involved in developing and implementing community programs in schools, churches, and health centers that promote positive lifestyle modifications (healthy food choices, increased physical activity, and achievement/maintenance of a healthy weight) for children and their families.

- The Diabetes Prevention Program conclusively showed that people can prevent the development of type 2 diabetes by making changes in food intake and increasing physical activity. A 5-10% decrease in body weight and 30 minutes/day of moderate physical activity produced a 58% reduction in diabetes.

DO'S AND DON'TS IN MAINTENANCE OF DIABETES

Do's

- Always prefer fresh and thoroughly washed vegetables (Salads) in your daily diet.
- Follow regular timings while taking food.
- Prefer whole wheat, whole grain, and unpolished rice.
- Low fat milk is constantly preferred.
- Obtain raw onion, freshly crushed garlic and cinnamon in your daily diet.
- Try to take limited servings of citrus fruits or guava every day.
- Prefer herbal tea, green tea as compared to caffeinated tea.

Don'ts

- Do not over eat at any time, avoid taking junk foods.
- Avoid sugar containing substances.
- Please be cautious while putting salt into own food preparations.
- Avoid fried and fatty foods, instead prefer boiled and steam cooked foods.
- Limit taking coffee or tea (2 cups).
- Keep away from taking cheese high in fat.
- Limit your intake of rice and potatoes, these can elevate blood glucose levels.
- Prefer a vegetarian diet, stay away from meat and eggs.
- Avoid mangoes, sapotas and bananas.

Chapter 4

CARDIOVASCULAR DISEASES

A controlled carbohydrate lifestyle really prevents risk factors for heart disease.
— *Robert Atkins*

INTRODUCTION

Cardiovascular disease (CVD) is a group of diseases which is related to the heart and blood vessels. It comprises of coronary artery diseases such as angina and myocardial infarction which is commonly famous as a heart attack. Additionally, also includes hypertensive heart disease, stroke, rheumatic heart disease, atrial fibrillation, aortic aneurysms, cardiomyopathy, peripheral artery disease, congenital heart disease, endocarditis, and venous thrombosis.

Cardiovascular diseases are the foremost basis of death worldwide. These mortalities, at a given stage, from CVD are more familiar moreover have been growing in much of the developing world, while rates have declined in the majority of the developed countries due to awareness. More or less 80% of CVD deaths in males and 75% of in females are due to coronary artery disease along with stroke out of them greater part is of elder patient. In the USA 11% of people between 20 and 40 have CVD, while 37% ranging 40 and 60, 71% of people among 60 and 80, and 85% of public over 80 have CVD. The typical age of death from coronary artery disease in developed world is approximately 80 while it is around 68 in the developing countries. Disease onset is characteristically seven to ten years previous in men as compared to women.

Although cardiovascular diseases are largely preventable it remains the leading cause of deaths worldwide. There are also new dimensions to this alarming situation. Over the past two decades, deaths from CVDs have been declining within high income countries, but have increased amazingly at a faster rate in low- and middle-income countries. Both population wide measures and enhanced access to person healthcare interventions can result in a major decline in the health and socioeconomic load caused by these diseases with their risk factors. These interventions, which are confirmation based and cost effective, are described as best buys in the Global Status Report on Non-communicable Diseases (NCDs) 2010.

At this moment in time, public health services within developing countries are overstretched via increasing stress to deal with heart disease, stroke, cancer, diabetes in addition to chronic respiratory disease. At the same time, healthcare systems are let down by a replica based on hospital care paying attention on the treatment of diseases, often centered around high technology hospitals that offer extensive treatment for merely a small minority of society. Hospitals consume huge amounts of capital, and health ministry's possibly will spend more than half their budgets on handling services which depend on hospitals. As a result, a large proportion of people with high cardiovascular risk remain undiagnosed, and yet those diagnosed have inadequate right of entry to treatment at the primary healthcare level; while proof suggests two-third of premature deaths due to NCDs and CVDs can be prevented by primary anticipation and another one-third by civilizing health systems to act in response more effectively and justifiably to the healthcare requests of people with NCDs.

There are several cardiovascular diseases linking the blood vessels which are well-known as vascular diseases for instance:

(a) **Coronary Artery Disease:** It is also acknowledged as coronary heart disease in addition to ischemic heart disease.

(b) **Peripheral Arterial Disease:** It ailment of blood vessels that provide blood to the arms and legs.

(c) **Cerebrovascular Disease:** This includes disease of blood vessels that deliver blood to the brain (includes stroke).

There are also lots of cardiovascular diseases that involve the heart to name as follows:

(i) **Cardiac myopathy:** It is the presence of inefficient cardiac muscle, hypertensive heart disease which is a problem of the heart secondary to high blood pressure or hypertension.

(ii) *Pulmonary heart disease* involves a breakdown at the right side of the heart with respiratory system.

(iii) **Cardiac dysrhythmias :** It is lack of normal rhythm or abnormalities of heart rhythm.

(iv) **Endocarditis:** It is inflammation of the internal coating of the heart i.e. the endocardium. The structures mainly involved are the heart valves.

(v) **Myocarditis:** Inflammation of the myocardium which the muscular part of the heart.

(vi) **Congenital heart disease:** Malformations of heart arrangement present at the time of birth.

(vii) **Rheumatic heart disease:** In this type of complications, heart muscles as well as valves damage because of rheumatic fever caused by *Streptococcus pyogenes*, a group of A streptococcal infection.

HYPERTENSIVE HEART DISEASE

The hypertension is defined as abnormally high blood pressure (above 120/80 mm Hg) in the arteries. A constant rise in blood pressure of systemic arteries is recognized as hypertension. Usually, a mean arterial pressure greater than 110 mm Hg under resting circumstances is considered to be hypertensive; this level normally occurs when the diastolic blood pressure is greater than 90 mm Hg and the systolic pressure is above 135-140 mm Hg. Hypertension is usually a less warning sign, but increases the risk of various other cardiovascular diseases like stroke, heart attack as well as non-cardiovascular diseases similar to renal damage, end stage of renal failure, etc. The hypertension is typically divided into main three type and further their subtype as described below.

[A] **Primary Hypertension:** An increased peripheral resistance result in primary hypertension. It is further divided in to two types specifically: benign and malignant hypertension

[B] **Secondary Hypertension:** The different forms of secondary hypertension are cardiovascular hypertension, renal hypertension, endocrine hypertension, neurogenic hyper-tension.

Hypertension in Pregnancy: *The* hypertensive disorders at some point in pregnancy arise in women with pre-existing primary or secondary chronic hypertension. Hypertensive disorders during pregnancy carry risks for the woman and the baby remains one of the leading causes of maternal death. Hypertensive disorders during pregnancy may also result in substantial maternal morbidity. More recently, the long-term consequences for women identified with hypertension at some stage in pregnancy have become clear, in particular chronic hypertension and an increase in lifetime cardiovascular risk. Hypertensive disorders also carry a risk for the baby, stillbirths in infants without congenital abnormality occurred in women with pre-eclampsia *[It is a collective term used for or of pregnancy characterized by elevated blood pressure along with a large quantity of protein in the urine which might result due to organ failure].*

The contribution of pre-eclampsia to the overall preterm birth rate is substantial women in their first pregnancy will give birth before 34 weeks as a consequence of pre-eclampsia. The pregnant women should be made aware of the need to look for instant advice from a healthcare professional if they experience symptoms of pre-eclampsia. The symptoms include severe headache, problems with vision (such as blurring or flashing in front of the eyes), rigorous pain just under the ribs, nausea, sudden puffiness of the face, hands or feet etc.

Reducing the Risk of Hypertensive Disorders in Pregnancy

The women at high risk of pre-eclampsia are advised to continue on 75 mg of aspirin daily from 12 weeks until the birth of the baby. Women at high risk are either chronic kidney disease, or autoimmune disease for instance systemic lupus erythematosis or anti-phospholipid syndrome along with type 1 or type 2 diabetes chronic hypertension.

Management of Pregnancy with Chronic Hypertension

1. Tell women who take angiotensin-converting enzyme (ACE) inhibitors and angiotensin II receptor blockers (ARBs): that there is an increased risk of congenital abnormalities if these drugs are taken during pregnancy

2. To discuss other antihypertensive treatment with the healthcare professional responsible for managing their hypertension, if they are planning pregnancy.

3. In pregnant women with uncomplicated chronic hypertension aim to keep blood pressure lower than 150/100 mmHg.

SIGN AND SYMPTOMS

The signs indicative of cardiovascular situation and atherosclerosis includes:

- Pale, clammy look, skin rashes or unusual spots.
- Cyanosis (blue tinge to the skin), particularly in the extremities.
- Rapid or shallow breathing with irregular heart rate with enlarged heart (measured by placing hand on chest).
- High or low blood pressure.
- Swollen veins in the neck along with swelling in the feet and ankles, cool extremities.
- Sudden weakness, confusion, sudden and severe headache.
- Paralysis (an inability to move) or numbness of the face, arms, or legs, especially on one part of the body.
- Difficulty in talking or perceptive dialogue, dilemma seeing by one or both eyes.
- Problems in breathing, dizziness, trouble walking, loss of balance or co-ordination, and unexplained falls, even loss of consciousness.

Heart Disease Symptoms Caused by Abnormal Heartbeats:

- Fluttering in your chest
- Racing heartbeat (tachycardia)
- Sluggish heartbeat (bradycardia)
- Chest discomfort, Short breath
- Dizziness
- Fainting (syncope) or near fainting.

CAUSES

- Smoking, including second hand smoke.
- Elevated level of certain fats along with cholesterol.
- High amounts of sugar in the blood due to insulin resistance or diabetes.
- High blood pressure.
- Blood vessel inflammation.
- Elevated and modified LDL.
- Free radical caused by cigarette smoking.
- Elevated plasma homocysteine.
- Hypertension
- Diabetes mellitus
- Genetic alterations
- Infections by Herpes virus – *Chlamydia pneumonia.*

COMMON MYTHS AND MISUNDERSTANDINGS

- If you have heart disease, you need to take it easy.
- If you take a cholesterol lowering drug, you can eat anything.
- It is okay to have higher blood pressure when you are older.
- Diabetes would not cause heart disease if you take diabetes medication.
- You can lower your risk of heart disease with vitamins and supplements.
- If you have smoked for years, you can not reduce your risk of heart disease by quitting.
- Heart disease is really a man's problem.
- If you have heart disease, you should eat as little fat as possible.
- A small heart attack is no big deal.
- Angioplasty and stenting or bypass surgery "fix" your heart.

RISK FACTORS OF CARDIOVASCULAR DISEASES

Tobacco: There are currently about one billion smokers in the world. Manufactured cigarettes symbolize the foremost form of smoked tobacco; other forms of tobacco consumed include "bidis" (a type of filter-less hand-rolled cigarette), cigars, hookahs and chewed tobacco. Tobacco use bears risks to health not only from direct consumption, but also from exposure to second-hand smoke. Nearly 6 million public die from tobacco use and exposure to second hand smoke annually throughout the globe. By 2030, tobacco associated deaths are estimated to increase by more than 8 million deaths annually. Smoking is anticipated to cause nearly 10% of CVD. There is an opposite correlation between income level and prevalence of tobacco use along with its related consequences. Additionally, tobacco consumption inflicts a larger harm with disadvantaged groups due to tobacco related illness and the impact on household expenditure. Therefore, interventions focusing on prevention of tobacco use, endorsement of smoke free environments and smoking termination should be vital components of national and international efforts to improve the health and well being of populations, especially the less wealthy community.

Physical Inactivity: Inadequate physical activity is defined as less than 5 times, 30 minutes of reasonable activity/week, or less than 3 times, 20 minutes of dynamic activity/week, or equivalent. People who are not sufficiently physically active bears a 20% to 30% increased risk of mortality compare to those who engage in as a minimum 30 minutes of reasonable physical action most days of the week. Many studies that have examined the association between physical activity and CVDs have reported reduced risk of death from coronary heart disease. Physical activity is a chief determinant of energy spending and thus basic to energy balance and weight control. The incidence of deficient physical movement is higher in high-income countries compared to low-income countries due to increased automation of work and use of vehicles. High-income nations have more than double the occurrence of insufficient physical activity compare to low-income countries for both men and women.

Physical activity improves endothelial function that enhances vasodilatation and vasomotor utility in the blood vessels. It also contributes to weight loss, glycaemic control, enhanced blood pressure, and improved lipid profile with better insulin sensitivity.

Harmful Use of Alcohol: The detrimental use of alcohol is a risk factor for manifold adverse health as well as social outcomes, including hypertension, acute myocardial infarction, cardiomyopathy, arrhythmia, hepatic cirrhosis and encephalopathy, pancreatitis, neuropathy, sexually transmitted diseases, unplanned pregnancy, violence, suicide and unintentional injuries (e.g. motor crashes). Additionally, citizens are affected by others drinking, together with their families, friends, co-workers and strangers. These troubles range in scale from noise and fear to physical abuse, sexual compulsion and social segregation.

The relationship between alcohol consumption and coronary heart disease along with cerebrovascular diseases is complex. It depends equally on the level and the pattern of alcohol consumption. There is a straight relationship among higher levels of alcohol consumption and the pattern of binge drinking (defined as 60 or more grams of pure alcohol per day) with the risk of CVD. Drinking at low levels devoid of episodes of profound drinking may be coupled with a decreased danger of many cardiovascular outcomes in some segments of the population. However, these effects tend to disappear if the patterns of drinking are characterized by heavy episodic drinking. Various mechanisms have been proposed for the protective effect of light to moderate alcohol consumption, including the beneficial effects of alcohol on the HDL cholesterol level, thrombolytic profile and platelet aggregation. In general, alcohol use is associated with multiple health risks that, at the population level, clearly outweigh potential benefits.

Unhealthy Diet: There is a substantial evidence about the dietary conditions of atherosclerosis and coronary heart disease in particular. Towering dietary intakes of saturated fat, trans-fat cholesterol and salt are related to cardiovascular risk. Obesity is a cardiovascular risk factor closely linked to diet and physical immobility. Obesity consequences, arises when there is an imbalance between energy intake and energy expenditure. The quantity of dietary salt consumed is an important determinant of blood pressure levels and overall cardiovascular risk. Everyday use of high-energy foods, such as process foods that are high in fats and sugars, promotes obesity compared to low-energy foods. A healthy diet can put in to a healthy body weight, a pleasing lipid profile as well as a desirable blood pressure. WHO recommends a population salt intake of less than 5 grams/person/day to help the prevention of CVD. However, data from different countries point out that the majority populations are consuming much more quantity of salt than this. It is expected that decreasing dietary salt intake from the current global levels of 9–12 grams/day to the suggested level of 5 grams/day would encompass a major impact on blood pressure and CVD. There is a direct link between the extent of salt reduction and the extent of blood pressure. High consumption of saturated fats and trans-fatty acids is linked to heart disease; removal of trans-fat and replacement of saturated fat with polyunsaturated vegetable oils lowers coronary heart disease risk .

Obesity: Obesity is strongly allied to major cardiovascular risk factors, for example, raised blood pressure, glucose intolerance, type 2 diabetes and dyslipidaemia. Risks of coronary heart disease, ischemic stroke and type-II diabetes mellitus increase steadily with an increasing body mass index (BMI). To achieve optimal health, the median BMI for adult populations should be in the range of 21–23 kg/m^2, while the goal for individuals should be to maintain a BMI in the range 18.5–24.9 kg/m^2. The prevalence of overweight in high-income and upper-middle income nations was more than double that of lower-middle-income countries. Rising income is associated with rising rates of overweight among infants and young children.

Raised Blood Sugar (Diabetes): Diabetes is a major risk factor of CVD. Diabetes is defined as having a fasting plasma glucose value $\geq$ 7.0 mmol/l (126 mg/dl). Impaired glucose tolerance and fasting glycaemia are threat categories for future growth of diabetes and CVD. The magnitude of diabetes and other abnormalities of glucose tolerance likely higher than the above approximation if the categories of "impaired fasting" and "impaired glucose tolerance" were included.

The estimated prevalence of diabetes is relative y consistent across the income groupings of countries. Low income countries shown the lowest prevalence, and the upper-middle-income nations shown the highest prevalence. The CVD accounts for about 60% of all mortality in people with diabetes. The risk of cardiovascular events is two to three times higher in citizens with type 1 or type 2 diabetes and the risk is disproportionately higher in women.

Diabetes has a poorer prognosis after cardiovascular events compared to people without diabetes. Furthermore, abnormal glucose regulation tends to occur together with other known cardiovascular risk factors such as elevated blood pressure, low HDL cholesterol, a high triglyceride level etc. A lack of early detection and care for diabetes results in severe complications, including heart attacks, renal failure, strokes, amputations and blindness. Primary concern to measurement of blood glucose and cardiovascular risk assessment as well as essential medicines including insulin can improve health outcomes of people with diabetes.

Raised Blood Cholesterol: The lipoprotein profile includes: (i) Low Density Lipoprotein cholesterol (LDL), also called "bad" cholesterol; (ii) High Density Lipoprotein cholesterol (HDL), commonly known as "good" cholesterol; and (iii) triglycerides. The surplus calories in the body are transformed into triglycerides and stored in fat cells all over the body. The LDL cholesterol is deposited in the walls of arteries and causes atherosclerosis. In common, lower LDL cholesterol numbers are better for vascular health. The HDL cholesterol protects against vascular disease by removing the "bad" cholesterol out of the arteries. Total blood cholesterol is a measure of LDL cholesterol, HDL cholesterol as well as other lipid components. High triglycerides raise the risk of atherosclerotic CVD. Raised blood cholesterol increases the risk of heart disease and stroke. Globally, one third of ischaemic heart disease is attributable to high cholesterol. Lowering raised serum cholesterol decreases the risk of heart disease. For example, a 10% fall in serum cholesterol in 40 years old men result in a 50% reduction in heart disease within five years; the same serum cholesterol drop for 70 years old men can result in a standard 20% reduction in heart disease occurrence within five years. The prevalence of raised total cholesterol evidently increases according to the income level of the country.

Social Determinants and CVDs: Societal determinants such as the distribution of income or the level of education obliquely influence cardiovascular health and health in general. These determinants shape a set of socioeconomic positions within hierarchies of supremacy, prestige and access to resources. Several structural mechanisms are responsible for creating the differential social positions of individuals, together with governance, education systems, labour market structures and the presence or absence of redistributive welfare policies. Social stratification shapes individual health status as well as CVD outcomes by impacting behavioral and metabolic cardiovascular risk factors, psychosocial status, living conditions and the health system.

The deprived, have limited opportunities for healthy choices and have a high prevalence of smoking. To mount an effective response to address social determinants that impact health, governance and systems need to be put in place that deliver a wide range of inter sectoral actions. Enhancing input and leadership of civil society groups in decision making are main aspects of the governance needed for action on social determinants. Such a comprehensive and responsible advance would throw in to the achievement of logical policies that increases opportunities for people and creates a healthier population.

LIFESTYLE MANAGEMENT IN CARDIOVASCULAR DISEASES

The importance of nutrition in modifying the risk of CVD has been repeatedly emphasized. Historically, the role of dietary components has been the predominant focus; however, foods are typically ingested in combinations fairly than individually. Over the past few years, rising attention has been given to dietary patterns and their relationship to health outcomes such as CVD.

- **End smoking:** If you smoke, quit. If someone in your household smokes, support them to quit. We know it is hard. But it is tougher to recover from a heart attack or stroke or to live with chronic heart disease. Commit to quit.

- **Restricting Salt Intake:** High dietary sodium intake is associated with an increased incidence of stroke, and with increased risk of death due to coronary heart disease or cardiovascular disease. Reducing dietary sodium with roughly 1700 mg (75 mmol) per day can lower systolic blood pressure by 4–5 mm Hg in hypertensive persons and 2 mm Hg in normotensive persons. This may reduce the need for antihypertensive drugs. Responses vary between individuals and are generally greatest among the elderly and those with severe hypertension. There is weak evidence suggestive of that weight loss combined with reduced dietary sodium may be more effective at lowering blood pressure than salt avoidance alone.

- **Dietary Potassium:** Some clinical trials suggest that increasing dietary potassium by approximately 2100 mg (54 mmol) per day can reduce systolic reduced salt diets along with thiazide diuretics may influence elderly patients to hyponatraemia, so electrolytes should be monitored regularly. Potassium enrich foods, such as bananas, kiwi fruit, avocado, potatoes (with skin), nuts and yoghurt, are more helpful in reducing blood pressure as compared to exposure of toxic potassium supplements. High potassium eating can produce hyperkalaemia in person with impaired renal function. It should be recommended only for those with known normal renal function.

- **Alcohol:** Evidence for benefits of light drinking has been challenged by a recent meta-analysis. Regardless of this debate, confirmation is emerging that all levels of alcohol drinking cause a rise in blood pressure. Reasonable drinking can increase blood pressure, while binge drinking appears to boost the risk of hypertension.

Epidemiological data illustrate a linear relationship among alcohol consumption and hypertension incidence. Reducing alcohol use can lower systolic blood pressure by an average of 3.8 mm Hg in patients with hypertension.

- **Physical Activity:** It is obvious that physical movement decreases resting as well as day time ambulatory blood pressure. In hypertensive individuals, standard aerobics decreases the systolic blood pressure by means of a typical of 6.9 mm Hg and diastolic blood pressure near 4.9 mm Hg. Regular physical activity has an independent cardio protective effect. Usual exercise is allied with an increase in HDL cholesterol along with reductions in body mass, waist circumference, percentage of body fat, insulin resistance, systemic vascular resistance, and plasma noradrenaline and plasma renin activity. This all collectively shows an improved outcome for management of hypertension related crises.

- **Body Weight:** There is a direct association between blood pressure and body weight and abdominal adiposity; some of the recent studies demonstrate that clinically noteworthy blood pressure reductions can be attained by modest weight loss in people with and without hypertension and that blood pressure reduction is proportional to weight loss. Each of 1% decrease in body weight lowers systolic blood pressure by a typical of 1 mm Hg. Weight decline confers a variety of other cardiovascular health benefits with reduced insulin resistance and hyperlipidaemia, in addition to reduced risk of left ventricular hypertrophy and obstructive sleep apnoea.

- **Choose Good Nutrition:** A healthy diet is one of the best weapons you have to fight against cardiovascular disease. The amount and type of food we eat can affect additional controllable risk factors: cholesterol, blood pressure, diabetes and overweight. Prefer nutrient rich foods that contain vitamins, minerals, fibre along with other nutrients but are lower in calories over nutrient-poor foods. Select a diet that insists intake of vegetables, fruits, and whole grains; including low-fat dairy products, non-tropical vegetable oils, and nuts; poultry, fish, legumes, as well as intake of sweets, sugar-sweetened beverages, and red meats must be limited. In order to sustain a healthy weight, co-ordinate your diet with your physical activity level so you are using up as many calories as you take in.

- **High Blood Cholesterol:** Fat blocked in our arteries is a disaster waiting to take place. Nearer or later it could trigger a heart attack or stroke. You have to trim down the intake of saturated fat, trans fat and cholesterol. If diet with physical activity only does not get those numbers downward, then medication may be the solution.

  Total Cholesterol: the total cholesterol score can calculated as (HDL + LDL + 20 per cent of our triglyceride level).

Low density lipoprotein (LDL) cholesterol ("bad" cholesterol): Low level of LDL cholesterol is measured healthy for our hearts fitness. For patients taking statins, the guiding principle say they do not need to get LDL cholesterol levels down to a specific target number. Lifestyle factors like a high diet in saturated and trans fats can lift LDL cholesterol.

High density lipoprotein (HDL) cholesterol = "good" cholesterol: The higher levels of HDL (good) cholesterol, are typically better. Small HDL cholesterol puts your heart at higher risk for disease. People with high blood triglycerides generally also have lesser HDL cholesterol. Genetic factors, type 2 diabetes, smoking, overweight and being inactive can all result in lower HDL cholesterol.

- **Triglycerides:** Triglyceride is the most common type of fat in the body. Standard triglyceride levels differ by age and sex. A high triglyceride level collectively with low HDL cholesterol or high LDL cholesterol is associated with build-up of fatty deposits in artery walls that increases the danger for heart attack and stroke.

- **Reduce Stress:** Some of the report noted a relationship between coronary heart disease risk and stress in a person's life. This may affect the risk factors for heart disease and stroke. For instance, people under stress may over eat; start smoking or over smoke than regular routine, research has even shown that stress reaction in young adults predicts middle-age blood pressure risk.

DO'S AND DON'TS

Do's

- Stop smoking, eat healthy foods, and drink less alcohol.
- Maintain a healthy weight.
- Increase physical activity – Plan for at least 30 minutes or more of moderate intensity physical activity every day of the week.
- Have a regular health check; Take your medications as directed by your doctor.

Don'ts

- Tobacco chewing, Cigarette smoking.
- Alcohol drinking, High salt intake.
- High Dietary potassium, Unhealthy diet.
- Physically Inactive, Stress.

Chapter-5

OBESITY

"Our food should be our medicine and our medicine should be our food."

— Hippocrates

INTRODUCTION

When body's, extra fat of a person accumulated to the level that it may cause an adverse effect on health, then the condition in medical term known as obesity. It is obtained by dividing weight of person by the square of the individual's height. It is defined by body mass index (BMI) and further evaluated in terms of fat allocation via the waist–hip ratio and total cardiovascular risk factors. BMI is very much interconnected to both percentage body fat as well as total body fat.

Obesity enhances the possibility of various diseases, mainly heart disease, obstructive sleep apnea, type-II diabetes, certain types of cancer, and osteoarthritis. It is most usually caused by an amalgamation of excessive food energy intake, lack of physical activity, along with genetic susceptibility, however in a few cases it may primarily caused by genes, endocrine disorders, medications, or psychiatric illness. There are little evidences to support the fact that some people eat little yet gain weight due to a slow metabolism. Normally, obese people have greater energy expenditure than their thin counterparts due to the energy required to maintain an increased body mass.

Dieting and exercising are the key treatments and management aspect for obesity. Diet feature can be enhanced by decreasing intake of energy dense foods, such as those high in fat along with sugars, and by escalating the eating of fibre. With an appropriate diet, anti-obesity drugs may be taken to decrease appetite or diminish fat absorption. If diet, workout, and medication are not efficient, a gastric balloon may aid with weight loss, or surgery performed to trim down stomach volume and/or bowel length, leading to sensation of full earlier and a reduced ability to absorb nutrients from food.

Obesity is a foremost avoidable cause of death globally, with increasing rates in adults and children. It is one of the mainly severe public health problems of the 21st century. It is stigmatized in much of the modern world, though it was extensively seen as a representation of wealth, it has been recently i.e. In 2013, classified obesity by the American Medical Association.

In earlier historical periods obesity was rare, and it was attainable only by small elite, even though by now well-known as a problem for health. But as wealth increased in the near the beginning Modern period, it affected increasingly larger groups of the population. In 1997, the WHO officially accepted obesity as a global pandemic. As of 2008 the WHO estimates that at least 500 million adults (greater than 10%) are obese, with higher rates among women as compared to men. The pace of obesity also increases by age at least up to 50 or 60 years old and is escalating faster than the overall rate of obesity.

Once measured a problem merely of high-income countries, obesity rates are increasing worldwide and affecting both the developed and developing world. These increases have been felt most spectacularly in metropolitan settings. Weight gain usually occurs over a time, most of the peoples be acquainted with when they have gained weight. Some of the signs of overweight or obesity includes:

- Feeling clothes tight and need a bigger size.
- Having extra fat around the waist.
- A higher than normal body mass index and waist circumference.

BMI is defined as the subject's weight divided by the square of their height and is calculated as follows.

$$BMI = \frac{m}{h^2}$$

Where, m and h are the subject's weight and height respectively. BMI is frequently expressed in kilograms per square metre, resulting when weight is measured in kilograms and height in metres. The most generally used definitions, recognized by the World Health Organization (WHO) in 1997 and published in 2000; provide the values listed in Table 3.1.

Table 3.1: Body mass index classification

BMI (kg/m^2)		Classification
From	up to	
-	18.5	Underweight
18.5	25.0	Normal weight
25.0	30.0	Overweight
30.0	35.0	Class I obesity
35.0	40.0	Class II obesity
40.0	-	Class III obesity

Some alterations to the WHO definitions have been made by particular bodies. The surgical literature breaks down "class III" obesity into further categories whose exact values are still disputed.

- Severe obesity is any BMI $\geq$ 35 or 40 kg/m^2.
- Morbid obesity is a BMI of $\geq$ 35 kg/m^2 and experiencing obesity-related health conditions or $\geq$ 40–44.9 kg/m^2.
- Super obesity is a BMI of $\geq$ 45 or 50 kg/m^2.

As Asian populations develop negative health consequences at a lower BMI than Caucasians, some nations have redefined obesity; the Japanese have defined obesity as any BMI greater than 25 kg/m^2 while China uses a BMI of greater than 28 kg/m^2.

COMMON MYTHS AND MISUNDERSTANDINGS

- If you are obese, blame your genes.
- If you are obese, you lack self-control.
- Lack of access to fresh fruits and vegetables is responsible for the obesity epidemic.
- The problem is not that we eat too much, but that we are too sedentary.
- We can conquer obesity through better education about diet and nutrition.
- Our child may appear overweight as per the growth charts, but our whole family is 'big boned.' So I do not believe he has a weight trouble at all.
- Because my child is heavy, he actually needs to eat more food to stay healthy.

The obese more likely to develop a number of severe fitness problems, together with:

- High triglycerides and low high-density lipoprotein cholesterol, heart disease, high blood pressure, cancer, including cancer of the uterus, cervix, ovaries, breast, colon, rectum, gall bladder, oesophagus, liver, pancreas, kidney and prostate.
- Breathing disorder, counting sleep apnea. a serious sleep disorder where breathing frequently stops and starts.
- Gynecological problems, such as infertility in addition to irregular periods.
- Erectile dysfunction as well as sexual health issues.
- When fat builds up in the liver and can cause inflammation condition is called as non-alcoholic fatty liver.
- Food makes you fat, high protein diet can help to lose weight.
- Exercise is the only solution to obesity.
- Stress has no effect on weight.

FACTS ABOUT OBESITY

- Healthy fats and oils are essential. The fats and oils consists of range essential fatty acid that helps us to maintain a healthy weight and to keep body functioning properly.

o Conjugated linoleic acid is an essential fatty acid, once revealed to build muscle mass, control metabolism and reduce chronic swelling. We get it from raw butter, meat and dairy products from grass fed cattle's.

o Coconut oil is another healthy fat, rich in essential fatty acids and ideal for cooking. It is anti-fungal, anti-viral and stimulates thyroid that regulates our metabolism.

o Certain foods can contribute to weight gain, but the real key is your *digestion*. Weak digestion and toxins create an acidic surroundings in body where pathogenic microorganisms (like yeast, bacteria and fungi) can thrive, making us sick and leading to weight gain. Microorganisms (microflora) that live in your intestines and keeps you healthy and strong.

o These microflora helps to digest food, strengthen immune system, and keep us safe from parasites and other pathogens in our food. They literally make vitamins (B5 and K) inside body, Feven help to maintain a normal weight.

o Excess protein eating is associated with health risks including heart disease, stroke, osteoporosis, kidney stones, plus elevated levels of ammonium in the female reproductive tract that lead to difficulty conceiving. Try to seek equilibrium in your diet, emphasizing land and/or marine vegetables, with a focus on raw, vegetables to progress digestion and vitality.

o Around 80% of our food should be land or ocean vegetables with the other 20% being protein or grain though, the query is not just how much *protein* we eat, it is about whether and the way we digest protein. Most people do not have enough stomach acid to digest protein, creating toxins in their body and setting the stage for illness, aging and weight gain.

o In addition to Exercise a healthy eating and lifestyle behavior show the way to balance in everything, including weight. Vigorous exercise can diminish visceral fat, the type of fat that surrounds our vital organs and causes inflammation, elevated blood sugar and weight gain.

o Standard work out burns hazardous visceral fat stimulates colon and enhances elimination. Deep breathing during aerobic exercise also releases carbon dioxide; aid in alkalizing blood and can reduce stress.

o Discover an exercise schedule that you enjoy and do it habitually as part of our healthy weight safeguarding, in addition to well diet and lifestyle practice, like getting plenty of revitalizing sleep.

o Chronically stressed people incident weight gain, abdominal obesity, type II diabetes, and cardiovascular disease more commonly than low stressed people.

Causes

Personally, a combination of excessive food energy intake and a lack of physical activity are consideration to elucidate most cases of obesity. An inadequate number of cases are due to principally genetics, medical reasons, or psychiatric illness. In contrast, increasing rates of obesity at a community stage are felt to be because of simply accessible and pleasant diet, increased reliance on cars, and mechanized manufacturing.

As societies become increasingly dependent on energy dense, big portions, in addition to fast-food meals, the connection between fast-food consumption and obesity becomes more concerning. Fast food culture is raising tendency among younger age group. The geared up accessibility, taste, low cost, promotion strategies and peer force make them admired within children and adolescents. These fast food hotels are in place to maximize the pace, competence and conformity. The menu is kept limited and standardized essentially to curtail the waiting moment so that the clients eat rapidly and go. This outlook delineates the budding fast food culture in India, its bang on children and strategies to counter act it need to develop strongly.

CHILDHOOD OBESITY IN INDIA

Today, India has large diabetics than any other nation on the planet, and will soon turn into the chief cause of death in our country. Indians, as a racial group are mainly at high threat for insulin resistance (syndrome X) and central obesity, both forerunners of diabetes, coronary heart disease as well as other 'life style' diseases. It is now rising influentially that these disorders begin in childhood (or even former, in fetal days), and apparent due to relations and build-up of a variety of risk factors, during life course. Pediatricians, thus, have a vital role in the prevention and control of the 'epidemic'. It is certainly ironic that a crisis of "plenty" viz., childhood obesity, has emerged while we are still fighting under nutrition and communicable disease.

In children, the difference between the rich and the poor is fairly evident in recently conducted urban studies. The prevalence of overweight (including obese) adolescents ranged from 22% in better off schools to 4.5% in lesser income cluster schools. In the capital of India i.e. Delhi school with tution fees more than ₹ 2,500/month, the occurrence of obese was 31%, of which 7.5% were bluntly overweight. In Pune, the figures for flabby children are 24% in a well off school and 6% in a 'corporation' school (unpublished data).

Measurement of obesity Body weight is reasonably correlated with body fat, and highly allied with height. Therefore, weight adjusted for height squared [body mass index (BMI in kg/m^2)] is a use key to judge overweight and is a quite dependable surrogate for adiposity. It is calculated easily from weight and height and it correlates with other measures of body fatness in kids as well as adolescents. The BMI moreover correlates with markers of secondary complications of obesity, including current blood pressures, blood lipids and with long-term mortality. A limitation factor of BMI is that it can't differentiate the obese individual from a muscular. It also cannot locate the site of fat, for example: people with 'central obesity' may have normal BMIs. In spite of numerous restrictions, BMI as of currently appears to be the most convenient way of measuring and comparing obesity for clinical and epidemiological purposes.

REFERENCE CHARTS FOR BMI CHILDREN

The BMI standards for adults are age independent in addition to that it is similar for both sexes. On the other hand in children, BMI changes physiologically with age and sex. At birth the middle BMI is as low as 13 kg/m^2, escalating to 17 kg/m^2 at age 1, falling to 15.5 kg/m^2 at age 6, then increasing to 21 kg/m^2 at age 20. Many countries have published BMI for age charts in support of their inhabitants, and some also have definite cut-off points on these charts to describe overweight and obesity. Recently, new BMI standards in children using a large worldwide representative sample from six diverse countries (not India), with widely differing frequency rates for obesity have been made available in form of publication. Age- and sex-specific BMI cut-off points for defining overweight and obesity in child have been resulting by identifying proportions in children analogous to adult BMIs of 25 kg/m^2 and 30 kg/m^2, respectively. These are referred to as IOTF end points and are now suggested as standards for international comparison of data.

CAUSES OF THE EPIDEMIC IN INDIA PERSPECTIVE

In India, there is a tremendous 'Urban/ Rural' and 'Rich / Poor' divide, incidence in the urban rich being much elevated than in countryside areas and poor communities. The causes include; change in lifestyle 'urbanization' by civilizing standards of living, and accessibility of food in abundance, the upper class societies of India in recent years have urbanized to western levels.

The components of change in lifestyles are:

➢ **Detrimental Eating Patterns, Incorrect Choices of Food:** Conventional micronutrient rich foods are being replaced by energy dense highly processed, micronutrient poor foods with very much enlarged portions 'Dil Mange More'. Soaring calorie refreshments, junk food revolution, cool cola ('thanda matlab') colonisation, and food as rewards or demonstration of be in love with all elements of new life styles. All partying and festivals appear to be centered on rich foods.

➢ **Sedentary Pursuits:** TV and movie watching, video games, internet gazing and telephone rumor sessions are now central activities of children. TV as well affects by heavy selling of colas and added fatty foods. The number of TV sets and telephone connections are touted as indices of progress.

➤ **'Obesogenic Schools' and Tution Course:** An important issue for obesity in India is the intense competition for admissions to schools and colleges with flourishing tuition classes right from nursery levels! Children are forced to use their play time for additional studies. Games or physical training sessions are limited or missing in many schools. A few schools do not have any playgrounds at all.

➤ **Insufficient Play Areas:** Owing to unsafe transportation (traffic, crime) children are discouraged from walk on streets or go to school by a cycle. Instead motorized vehicles are admired and they are perceived to be quicker in addition safe for transport. Scarcities of open spaces for work out and short of parental time to oversee play are all part of new pro-obesity lifestyles. As against food as rewards, ironically exercise is meted out as a punishment - '100 sit ups,' 'run round the field.'

Genetic 'Constitutional' predisposition the factors responsible are as follows:

➤ Modern environment may have unmasked previously silent obesogenic genes thrifty genotypes.

➤ Programming of formerly malnourished populations to build-up fat more intensely in an effort to store for future starvation ('early life origins').

➤ Stunting in childhood (short height for age) may increase the risk of central obesity especially in transitional economies.

➤ High rate of gestational diabetes in pregnant women causing higher birth weights in babies leading to intergenerational effects of obesity in childhood and its attendant's problem.

➤ Familial pattern of eating, exercise and behavior.

Other factors includes: Extended and restricted breast feeding is related with an appreciably lower rate of obesity and hypertension in later life. It is not clear if early introduction of energy intense supplements during infancy has contributed to childhood obesity in India. High glycemic index of our mostly carbohydrate diet may be liable for hyperinsulinism, weight gain and eventual type 2 diabetes. Yet other factors controlling body weight guideline such as 'low body metabolic rate (BMR)' and possibly govern by hypothalamus, these factors as of now are all speculative.

Obesogenic lifestyle behaviors are less well cultivated in children and thus more willing to change. A devastating body of confirmation now indicates that avoidance must begin in childhood to diminish the burden and cost of obesity in society. In India, Public health efforts so far, have been directed towards improving nutrition. However, the solitary approach to cut short the growing epidemic appears to be anticipation of overweight and other lifestyle troubles in childhood itself. In order to overcome this epidemic, it has to take up as a challenge along with this requires strong social and political will in addition to medical management. An intensive public health approach will be required for effective prevention. The whole family, indeed the whole society must be targeted for the health of the future generation.

In India, we have just started about reporting high prevalence of obesity in children. Obviously then, no intervention studies have not been carried out as yet. Evidently, many lessons can be learnt from the successful as well as the not so successful programs in other countries. The subsequent strategies recommendations specifically for our nation are based on the above evidence as well as observational data.

STRATEGIES AND AIMS

Public Health Approach: As a Public Health Approach, fundamentally all kids, adolescents and families should profit from counseling to avert excess weight gain and obesity.

Lifestyle Approach

(i)   **Healthy Eating Patterns:** Emphasis should be on nutrition relatively than 'dieting'. It is imperative to keep healthy workings of traditional diets (i.e., micronutrient rich food such as fruits, vegetables and whole grain cereals) and guard next to heavily marketed energy dense fatty and salty foods (e.g., prepackaged snacks, ice-creams and chocolates), and the sugary cold drinks. The strategy should be to recognize and eliminate danger features of high calorie intake for instance frequent snacking (samosas, potato chips, chiwdas), eating out regularly (burgers, dosas), celebrate with food (cake, chocolates) moreover drinks (colas, beers, soda etc.). Healthier alternatives can be suggested. Habits attained early have more chance of remaining throughout life. A simple Indianised message could be "think of a day's food composition as a 'Thali' wherein 50% (half) is full of vegetables, salads and fruits. A quarter (25%) should be portion of cereals such as rice or chapattis and residual quarter should be protein based (dal/milk/egg/animal protein)". Fried, snacks and 'sweet dishes' are only for a very few special occasions.

(ii)   **Increase Physical Activity Levels:** Children should be encouraged to be active not only for weight control but for general well being. Many adolescents/pre-adolescents may feel defined physical exercises (aerobics, treadmills) boring and disciplinary. Alongwith, it they are more likely to keep on doings if it is incorporated compulsorily to their daily routines, e.g., walking or cycling near school and spending time on ground for sports with friends. The WHO insists as a minimum 30 minutes of increasing moderate exercise (equivalent to walking briskly) for all ages, whereas in children, an extra 20 minutes of dynamic exercise (equivalent to running), three times in a week. In broad-spectrum, modest to forceful activities for a period of minimum one hour daily may be a more practical recommendation for all school going children.

(iii) **Decrease Sedentary Behavior:** Possibly even more essential is diminishing sedentary activities. In our country, chief sedentary behaviors are television (should be restricted to no more than 2 hours a day), computers, telephone conversations and importantly tuition classes (restriction may not be possible).

(iv) **Avoid overfeeding underdeveloped populations.** Evaluate physique and prevent feeding excess calories to children with low weight for age except regular weight for height i.e., 'stunted children'. Most primary epidemic management and prevention programs (school mid day meals) employ food supplements that gives sufficient energy and protein but may be poor in micronutrients. Such programs may induce weight gain in underweight children while length deficit may not be reversed, thereby creating a risk for obesity. Quality of foods provided in 'feeding programs' is crucial fruits and vegetables should be included and energy excess should be avoided.

(v) **'Target' populations most in need of interventions:** In India, this would most likely represent urban children from higher and mid socio economic position. Targeting avoids confusing message heading for opposite segments of the general public.

(vi) **'Modify the approach'** to go well with the specific needs of the population. Use culture appropriate messages e.g., urban Indians need to know that 'chubby' or fat child is not equivalent to 'healthy' babies.

(vii) **Make a deal with 'Behavior' Change:** Behavior or deeds are in fact culture based. Consider socio-cultural and ethnic issues, these would be important in suggesting diets and activity. For example, adolescent girls belonging to traditional families are often disheartened from playing outdoor games but can be encouraged to perform physical household chores.

(viii) Focus on involvement of entire family (parents, grandparents) indeed the entire community for better results. Average Indian families have poor knowledge of 'healthy eating'.

SPECIAL STRATEGIES TO TARGET SPECIFIC AGE GROUPS

Infants and Young Children

- Mothers should avoid surplus weight gain in pregnancy; control diabetes or impaired glucose tolerance in pregnancy.
- Endorse exclusive breast feeding for six months.
- Avoid putting sugars, starches or oils to feeding formulae.
- Ensure suitable micronutrient intake especially of iron, calcium along with vitamins.

- Monitor growth and weight for height and BMI.
- Make clear differentiation of 'catch up growth' from accelerated weight gain. Catch up development should be coupled with gain in height relative to weight gain.
- Educate mothers to recognize the child's appetite and not to force feed.
- Instruct families that 'fat infants create fat adults'.

Children and Adolescents

The fat jump back age (5-8 years) and adolescences are mainly high risk periods for accumulating fat. Strategies for prevention consists of encourage active lifestyles together with not less than one hour of energetic 'play' per day. Limit TV and other sedentary activities to Educate about the evils of alcohol/tobacco to adolescents.

Channels of interventions based programs, schools are most likely the perfect medium of intercession as they are fundamental to children's lives with information can be comparatively quickly dissolute from side to side this channel. Various aspects to be measured are:

- Preparation of teachers in lifestyles, nutrition and activity.
- Introduction of ideal school meals or provision of canteens offering only healthy choice depending upon Indian foods.
- The start of 'nutrition and physical education' in school curriculum. Such activities should become compulsory and/or a 'scoring subject' with marks to be added to total grades. Then only parents/students will give the required attention and time in academics.
- After the school games (supervised/unsupervised) to be encouraged. School playgrounds should kept open on weekends and holidays.
- Overweight children should not be targeted, or teased, hence engage parent associations.
- School health checkups should check BMI along with height and weight once a year. Media participation another dominant channel particularly for upper along with middle class societies is media coverage. Usually columns, articles and supplements in newspapers have by now started leaving a mark.
- It is important for doctors and other health professionals to think 'prevention of obesity' at all visits and incorporate relevant health education. The success of this channel in current time with, immunizations, breast feeding and prevention of malnutrition makes this an optimistic channel for such a promotion.
- Include BMI charts and waist circumference (besides height, weight and head circumference) in routine health report. Keep an eye on BMI annually, specifically for children from the families of high risk possibility.

- Identify children with BMI > 75% for recurrent monitoring and 'life style' modifications.
- Parent's fascination with food intake and pleas for tonics should be discouraged. Governmental establishment both health and infrastructural authorities should be responsible for:
- Designing national policies.
- Promoting food outlets/restaurants to provide healthy options.
- Providing opportunities for safe work out.

Regulate advertisements aimed at children and insist on food labeling. Think taxation on 'fatty food' or alternatively reduce taxation/promote production of fresh food and vegetables. As said formerly this kind of a Public Health Approach needs strong social as well as political will with concurrent medical motivation and management.

MANAGEMENT OF ESTABLISHED OBESITY

Diet schedule may produce weight loss over the short term, but keeping this weight loss is often difficult and regularly required to exercise along with low food energy diet. All types of low-carbohydrate and low-fat diets come into sight evenly beneficial. Similar risks are related with obesity for different diets that contributing to heart disease and diabetes. The lifestyle changes can make you sure for maintenance of weight ranging from 2–20% of long-term. The nutritional changes and lifestyle are effective in limiting excessive weight gain during pregnancy and improve outcomes in support of both the mother and the baby. Intensive behavioral counseling is recommended for both obese as well as other individual having risk factors for heart complications.

The extensive availability of nutritional plan has done little to tackle the problems of overeating and reduced dietary option. At the same time, an increase occurred in the average amount of food energy consumed. Most of this extra food energy came from an increase in carbohydrate consumption rather than fat consumption. The main sources of these additional carbohydrates are sweetened beverages and potato chips that account for almost 25% of daily food energy in young adults. The utilization of sweetened drinks for instance soft drinks, fruit drinks, iced tea, along with energy and vitamin water drinks thought to be having positive impact in intensifying obesity and increased risk of metabolic syndrome.

When the public health promotion is to be targeted to the general public as a whole, individual or clinic based approach is necessary for the treatment of the obviously obese child. A guideline for assessment by pediatricians in their clinic should be provided.

Principles of therapy are outlined in the following section.

Management of Obesity Clinic: Management of established obesity in children needs a rigorous and a persistent effort from a team of veteran health professionals. Treatment is more likely to be successful in children than adults. Western guidelines by and large apply to our clinics and are outlined below.

Approach to therapy Medical Goal

Medical goal should be resolution of complications and co-morbidities, for example, hypertension and hyperlipidemia.

Behavioral Goal: Achievement of healthy eating and activity patterns rather than accomplishment of perfect body weight.

Weight Goal: Weight safeguarding rather than weight loss in young kids, 'allow the child to grow up into his weight'. Stretched weight protection will allow a slow decline in the BMI as the child grows in height.

General Approach to Therapy: Institute small, gradual and stable changes, exercise programs designed at swift weight loss. Engage the family and all care givers in the conduct program. Intervention should start on before time (soon after age 3 years but before adolescence). Clinicians should encourage and empathize and not criticize.

Theoretically, obesity management is energy balance (eat less and exercise more). Conversely, in practice the management can be challenging and provoking because of repeated relapses. The principles of therapy are generally same as in prevention viz.:

(a) Reduced calorie eating

(b) Amplified activity levels

(c) Decreased sedentary performance

(d) Family participation

(e) Behavioral changes

Restrictive energy intake of developing children can result in reduced linear growth speed in obese children and is therefore risky. Dieting could also increase incidence of scarce nutrients, such as iron, calcium, zinc and vitamins A, C and E. An elevated degree of parental dietary control may in fact have adverse psycho behavioral effects on young children with treatment failures. So the aim should be provision of well balanced healthy meals with a strong approach to eat. A number of different dietary studies have shown unbeaten decline of calorie intake and enhanced eating behaviors. The advice typically centers on reducing calories from fat, saturated fats, cholesterol and sugars while escalating fruits, vegetables and whole grain cereals. Trials of hypocaloric diets, protein customized fasts, fibre supplementation and anorectic drugs have been revealed to ineffective in children during the long range.

Addition of physical action and drop in sedentary behavior, equally (supervised and unsupervised) improves long term outcome. The important components of behavioral therapy include treatment of families as a complete, recognition of problem behaviors and their alterations, and `tailor' made advice and support component. Parenting skills recommended in treatment plans are praising the child's behavior, never using food as reward, establishing hard daily family meal along with snack times, give only healthy option, eliminating temptations and being a good role model.

KEY MESSAGES

o India is in the midst of an escalating epidemic of lifestyle disorders associated with childhood obesity.

o The important causes of the epidemic in India appear to be: Unhealthy consumption patterns, compact physical activity, increased sedentary pursuits and perhaps "constitutional predispositions".

o Prevention must begin early in the form of a public health drive directed towards lifestyle change of the family / society as a whole. The promotion requires strong social and political will.

o Health professionals must think on 'prevention of obesity' at all visits, scrutinize BMI and guarantee that 'nutrition messages' are not confusing.

o Special strategies for different ages and channels of interventions for prevention of obesity have been outlined.

o Clinic based individual assessment of the obese child and principles of therapy are provided.

In India, media advertisement and publicity s underneath the authority of ministry of information and broadcasting (GOI). A commission has been set up by the ministry to review the complaints, make a decision whether the commercials violates the rules and issue a notice to television channels in evidence of infringement. Media rules and regulation are laid down under India Cable Television Network Act 1994 and Advertising Standard Council of India (ASCI). Guidelines related to quality of food products advertised in Indian medium should be immediately need to formulate. Some of the suggestions related to encouraging healthy food habits and decreasing unhealthy fast foods consumption in regular life among children's are outlined in below.

PROMOTING HEALTHY FOOD INTAKE IN CHILDREN

1. *Child should be offered with a plate filled with plenty of brightly coloured vegetables, fruits and sprouts.*

2. *Ice-cream, chocolates and other heavy desserts can be replaced by low fat fresh yogurt.*

3.   *Fresh lime juice, coconut water and fresh fruit juices should be preferred to sodas and soft drinks as beverages.*

4.   *Grilled sandwiches should be favored instead of fried. In the same manner when choice of baked, broiled, and grilled items of meat need to be select rather than fried or poultry.*

5.   *Avoid giving chocolate bars as gifts or reward to the children for their good habits or academic achievements.*

6.   *Limit the portion size of food prepared. Regular size meal possibly opted against 'mega meal offer' or 'combo meal offer'.*

7.   *While eating away from home, avoid opting for dishes with rich creamy layers and lots of spices.*

8.   *Replace naan with tandoori roti as low fat option breads in Indian menu.*

9.   *Serving dishes can be blend fried moderately than deep fry to decrease the fat content.*

10.   *Dough (aatta) used for preparing poori/pakoras should be broad and devoid of ghee or oil for making the bread as this might raise oil absorption.*

Fast food refers to food that can be delivered ready to eat. The terms fast food and junk food are habitually used interchangeably. The majority of the junk foods are fast foods as they are prepared and served fast, but not all fast foods are junk foods, particularly when they are geared up with nutritious filling. The definitions of various food items are described as bellow:

- **Fast Foods:** It is food sold in a restaurant or store which are burgers, pizzas, fries, hamburgers, patties, nuggets, in a packaged form for take away. These are rapidly prepared and quickly served Indian foods like pakora, samosa, namkeen etc.

- **Junk Food:** Energy thick foods with towering sugar/fat/salt content with low nutrient value in terms of protein, fibre, vitamin and mineral content. For example: Chips, chocolate, ice-cream, soft drinks, burgers, pizzas etc.

- **Instant Foods:** Foods that undergo special dispensation that is ready for serving once dispersed in a liquid with low cooking time. For example: noodles, corn flakes, soup powder,

- **Street Foods:** Ready to eat foods and beverages prepared and sold by hawkers or vendors in streets or other burgers. For example: Chaat, gol guppa, samosa, tikki, noodles, chowmein etc.

FACTORS RELATED TO FAST FOOD CONSUMPTION

Fast food chains are getting fame with small families as running parents have less time for meal groundwork at home. The vast majority of working parents with school going children are awkward with very tiring commutes, extra household responsibilities and stress. At the same time as their children spend most of their time away from home by attending tuition classes after their school hours or busy in recreational activity.

For children skip breakfast at home, fast food comes handy in school. A positive link of improved fast food consumption, skipped breakfasts in addition to increased body mass index was found among adolescents. The socio-economic status is main factor associated to fast food use among children. The children from high socio-economic status preferred fast foods to traditional foods regardless of their better nutritional knowledge. Proximity of fast food joints to households could also predispose to increased consumption.

FAST FOODS AND SCHOOL

Most of the schools in India have banned the sale of junk foods in the school cafeteria. Akshaypatra foundation, a non-governmental organization in India along with government aided schools has started school mid-day meal program, where healthy Indian foods are presented to children.

INDIAN FAST FOODS

India has affluent heritage of foods in addition to recipes. Trendy north Indian fast foods comprise aloo-tikki, bhel-puri, pani puri chaat, pakora, chole bhature, pav bhaji, dhokla, and samosa. The cooking method decides calorie and fat content in Indian fast food. Most of them are prepared by deep frying in fats especially trans fat and saturated fats. Foods that are baked, roasted or cooked in tandoor have lesser fat content. Hydrogenated oil in Indian cuisine is rich in trans fats and have been replaced by refined vegetable oil in many restaurants. The Indian fast food content of trans fat are much far higher than western foods. Trans fat content in bhatura, parantha, moreover puris are 9.5%, 7.8% and 7.6%, respectively as compared to 4.2% in regular French fries. South Indian dish like idli and uthappam are healthier as they are rich in carbohydrates and proteins rather than fat.

The present analysis represented that obesity rates in children and adolescents are increasing not only in the higher socio-economic society but also in the lower income groups where underweight is still a major anxiety. This indicates the need for a balanced and sensitive way to address nutrition as well as economic transitions to effectively tackle this double burden irony in India.

CONTRIBUTORS TO THE RECENT INCREASE OF OBESITY

(1)   Insufficient sleep.

(2)   Endocrine disruptors (environmental pollutants that obstruct the lipid metabolism).

(3)   Decreased inconsistency in ambient temperature.

(4)   Suppression of smoking, because smoking decreases the appetite.

(5) Increased use of medications that can cause weight gain (e.g., atypical antipsychotics).

(6) Comparative increases in ethnic and age groups that tend to be heavier.

(7) Late age pregnancy.

(8) Natural selection for higher BMI.

(9) Mating with same genotype partner (i.e. selection of similar genotype) leading to increased concentration of obesity risk factors (this would raise the number of obese people by growing population conflict in weight).

DO'S AND DON'TS IN OBESITY

Do's

- Shop for low-fat and low-calorie food items.
- Stock only healthy foods at home.
- Take everyday small meals to stay away from food cravings.
- Receive more proteins in diet in order to stay longer without food.
- Consult a certified professional before taking up any diet plan.
- Edify yourself regarding good food practice and balanced diet.
- Put healthy foods to diet e.g. oat meal, walnuts, salads.
- Use warm water for drinking.
- Control your craving for oily and fried foods, use vegetable oil.
- Eat lower calorie vegetables e.g. bitter gourd, drumstick etc.
- Go for a rapid morning walk of 30 minutes.
- Yoga and Meditation to manage your stress and fatigue.
- Eat a tomato every day in the morning.
- Embrace cabbage in daily meal. It will stop the alteration of sugars to fat.
- Eat Vitamin B_{12} sources.
- Favor steamed, boiled along with baked vegetable rather than fried.
- Keep away from 'alcohol'.
- Drink skimmed milk instead of intact milk.
- Go for roast, bake or boil meat moreover other protein source those have fat.
- Incorporate lemon in diet and drinks.

Don'ts

- Don't go for shopping if you are hungry.
- Don't keep on watching too much TV.

- Do not consider fraud super diets like – for weight loss any miracle foods, weight loss without exercise.
- Don't eat elevated carbohydrate vegetables e.g. potato etc.
- Do not take more sugary or sweet products.
- Do not go for fried and oily foods.
- Don't create sedentary habits, do not 'smoke'.
- Don't go for unnecessary sleep.
- Do not skip any meal.
- Do not drink less than 8-10 glasses of water daily.
- Do not eat more dairy products.
- Do not eat salty foods or meals.
- Don't consume oil or ghee, butter.
- Don't have high carbohydrate diet like rice etc. instead of that prefer cereals, oat meal.
- Do not over-eat or under-eat.

Chapter 6

ARTHRITIS

My message is keep moving. If you do, you will keep arthritis at bay.

— *Donna Mills*

INTRODUCTION

Chronic musculoskeletal diseases, in particular osteoarthritis (OA), Rheumatoid Arthritis (RA) and Low Back Pain (LBP) are the most important causes of disability adjusted life years in both developed and developing countries. As in most chronic diseases, lifestyle interventions play a very important role in the aetiology and management of chronic musculoskeletal disease. Arthritis is a type of joint disorder which comprises inflammation of one or more joints. There are over 100 different forms of arthritis. The most widespread type of arthritis is osteoarthritis and degenerative joint disease, as a consequence of distress to the joint, infection in the joint (septic arthritis), or other types of arthritis like rheumatoid arthritis, psoriatic arthritis, and related autoimmune diseases.

Arthritis is a chronic inflammatory condition, producing harm to joint mediated by cytokines, chemokines, and metallopro-teases. The disease is systemic, typically disturbing the synovial joints and meticulous synovial structures (bursae and tendon sheaths) in particular. This usually initiates with the small bones of hands in addition to foot. In advanced situations, most of the joints are exaggerated. The systemic nature of the situation means that several other organs may turn out to be occupied as the condition progresses. For instance extra-articular association can comprise symptoms and effects, for example : fever, weight loss, fatigue or weakness, swollen lymph nodes, anemia, nodules, dry eyes, fibrosis of lungs, liquefied chest cavity, vasculitis, neuropathy, GI, and kidney disease. The most important grumble of individuals who have arthritis is joint pain. Pain is often a constant and may be confined to a small area of affected joint. The pain from arthritis is due to inflammation that occurs around the joint. That damages joint from disease, daily wear and tear of joint, muscle strains causes by vigorous movements against stiff painful joints and fatigue.

The inflammation of arthritis is depending upon the inflammatory markers which infiltrate from the blood vessels to the tissue. Diagnosis is made by clinical examination from an appropriate health professional, and may be supported by other tests such as radiology and blood tests, depending on the type of suspected arthritis. The patient usually complains pain and patterns may differ depending on arthritis and location. Arthritis is generally worse in the morning and coupled with firmness; in the early conditions, patients regularly have no symptoms after a morning shower.

Even though a specific diet cannot heal arthritis, some people have institute that symptoms can get better through dietary changes. There are more than 100 variety of arthritis hence it is important to keep in mind that what may work for one person might not work for other.

For instance, inhabitants living with gout may decrease painful inflammation, also identified as a "flare," by not overwhelming large amounts of foods that augment uric acid levels (e.g., red meat and alcohol) and avoiding organ meats, while individuals with Rheumatoid Arthritis (RA) seem to gain from eating more omega-3 fats (e.g., found in Sardines and Salmon). The most vital link among our diet and arthritis is our weight. Mounting a healthy lifestyle that comprise eating nutritious, well balanced meals as well as being physically energetic will help to provide you with the energy you require to complete your everyday activities and handle your arthritis. And keep in mind, while a healthy diet is vital, you should not discontinue or alter your medical conduct devoid of discussing your plan with your healthcare team. While some people spin to nutritional supplements, often the same results can be attained through simply managing a healthy diet. It is also significant to think whether your usual diet is bountiful you all the imperative basic nutrients. If it does not, then your wide-ranging health will experience a consequence on the arthritis. Ask doctor to pass on you to a registered dietitian.

OSTEOARTHRITIS

Osteoarthritis (OA) is also known as "wear and tear" or degenerative arthritis, is one of the main frequent causes of arthritis that normally affects weight bearing joints (mostly knee and hip), but can also affect other joints in the body including the hands. At present is no precise portrayal of osteoarthritis, but for the purpose of this part is to view as the clinical and pathological outcome. That range from disorders result in structural and functional breakdown of synovial joints. Which results in loss and erosion of articular cartilage, subchondral bone modification, meriscal degeneration which is a synovial inflammatory reaction, bone and cartilage overgrowth. It can influence equally to the larger as well as smaller joints of the body, including hands, wrists, foot, back, hip, along with knee. The disease is essentially one acquired from daily wear and tear of the joint; on the other hand, it can also arise as a outcome of injury. In current years, some joint or limb deformities, such as knock-knee otherwise acetabular over coverage or dysplasia, have as well measured as a predisposing feature for knee or hip osteoarthritis. It begins within the cartilage along with ultimately causes the two divergent bones to erode hooked on each other. The circumstances starts with negligible pain at some point in physical motion, but soon the pain continuous even while in a state of rest. The pain can be unbearable and stop the person from commencing some normal activities also. Osteoarthritis classically affects the weight bearing joints, such as back, spine, and pelvis. More than 30% of women have a few degree of osteoarthritis by age 65. The general risk factors for OA are best understood as resulting from excessive mechanical stress that is applied to a susceptible or vulnerable joint. Increased age (> 40–50 years), genetic tendency, positive family history, ethnicity, female gender, and nutritional factors can increase the risk of a susceptible joint. The unwarranted mechanical tension can cause mal-alignment, muscle weakness, obesity and previous joint injury that altered the structural integrity of the joint.

RHEUMATOID ARTHRITIS

It is a disorder in which the body's own immune system starts to attack body tissues. The attack is not only directed at the joint but too many other parts of the body. In rheumatoid arthritis, the joint lining and cartilage majorly damage which ultimately consequences in erosion of two opposite bones. Rheumatoid arthritis over and over again affects joints in the fingers, wrists, knees along with elbows. The disease is symmetrical (appears on both sides of the body) and can lead to severe deformity in a few years if not treated. It occurs by and large in people aged 20 as well as if occurred in children, the disorder can present with a skin rash, fever, pain, disability, and restrictions in daily actions. Often, it is not clear why it occurred, with earlier diagnosis and aggressive treatment; many individuals can lead a well-mannered quality of life. The drugs to treat rheumatoid arthritis vary from corticosteroids to monoclonal antibodies given parentally. The most recent drugs like Remicade can considerably perk up quality of life in the short term. In very few conditions, surgery may be essential to replace joints but there is no cure for the poor health.

Clinical Manifestations

The medical manifestations include pain, swelling, plus tenderness of small joints of hands. It is crucial to take a thorough history of the joint symptom, particularly on the style of onset, how gradual or acute, the outline of joints concerned, and any discrepancy in symptoms as per time of day. Although it is a systemic syndrome, patients may thus have related symptoms similar to fever, weight loss, moreover fatigue.

Onset

The most frequent form of appearance is gradual and insidious is beginning of joint pain along with swelling, taking place for weeks to months. Some individual may present with an unexpected explosive arrival polyarthritis. Still some may present through temporary self-limited episodes of mono- or polyarthritis enduring days to weeks. This appearance is famous as palindromic rheumatism. It is typically a polyarticular disease however rarely it may represented as a monoarthritis; in such a circumstances more known causes of monoarthritis should be for all time feint out similar to infectious arthritis, gout, and spondyloarthritis.

Morning Stiffness

Morning rigidity (i.e. difficulty in moving around) lasting for 1 hour or more is a characteristic of RA. A parallel incident can arise if a patient is immobile for a period throughout the day. This is most likely due to the build-up of edema fluid surrounded by inflamed synovial tissues for the duration of sleep. The sunrise stiffness disappear as edema with products of inflammation are engrossed by lymphatics and venules and returned to normal circulation by motion associated the use of muscles and joints.

Joint Involvement

The joints nearly all usually concerned in RA are the wrists, small joints of the hands along with feet. Which includes the metacarpophalangeal joints, proximal interphalangeal joints of the finger; interphalangeal joints of thumbs, in addition to metatarsalphalangeal joints are regularly affected. Distinctively the distal interphalangeal joints are out of danger. As disease progresses, bigger joints like the ankles, knees, elbows, and shoulders often turn out to be affected.

The thoracic, lumbar and sacral spine are almost spared in RA. On the other hand, cervical spine participation is not rare, cervical spine association is seen in well-known RA. There can be atlantoaxial sub-luxation, that manifests as neck pain, but passive range of movement of the cervical spine is repeatedly normal. The temporomandibular joint and sternoclavicular joints are also concerned in varying extent.

Pattern of Arthritis

RA is a polyarthritis. Joint association is typically bilateral and balanced. The arthritis in RA is an "additive" type of arthritis, in that it is exceptional for symptoms to dispatch entirely in one set of joints whereas mounting in another. This is in dissimilarity to rheumatic fever where the arthritis is traveling, in that symptoms in one joint drop fully before relating another.

Asymmetrical joint connection is seen when RA coexists among poliomyelitis, meningioma, encephalitis, neurovascular syphilis, strokes, and cerebral palsy. Joints on the paralysed area are classically spared.

PREVALENCE

Incidence of OA in India is reported to be in the range of 17 to 60.6%. The reported prevalence of OA from a study in rural India is 5.78%. Most knee OA is managed by primary care physicians rather than rheumatologists. Planning Commission 2011, Osteoarthritis (OA) occurs in half of all chronic situation in persons aged over 65 with about 25% of cases over the age of 60 years have notable pain with disability instigating osteoarthritis. As per a current detail published regarding OA, over 40% of the Indian residents in the age fraction of 70 years or above experience OA. Almost 2% of these endure severe knee pain plus disability. As per a latest report quoted by Piramal Healthcare Limited in a countrywide promotion against chronic diseases, India is predictable to be the chronic disease capital, with 60 million people in the midst of arthritis, by 2025. The government, the medical fraternity, NGOs and private sector, should come simultaneously in opposition to the assault of chronic disease.

SIGN AND SYMPTOMS

Osteoarthritis: It may embrace joint pain along with progressive stiffness with the intention of develop regularly.

Rheumatoid arthritis: This may consist of painful inflammation, swelling, in addition to stiffness in the legs, fingers, arms and wrists happening in the similar joints on both sides of the body, especially upon awakening.

Infectious arthritis: It may incorporate fever, chills, joint inflammation, sharp pain that with tenderness, and are associated with an injury or infection in another place in body.

COMMON MYTHS AND MISUNDERSTANDINGS

- It is an old person's disease.
- Arthritis can be cured.
- Arthritis is caused by a poor diet.
- Arthritis consists of only minor aches and pains.
- "You felt all right yesterday....why so exhausted today?"
- Arthritis is induced by a cold and wet climate.

RISK FACTORS

The common risk factors in OA implicit as resulting from extreme mechanical pressure that is useful to a vulnerable or defenseless joint. Augmented age (> 40–50 years), genetic inclination, affirmative family record, ethnicity, female gender, in addition to nutritional factors can amplify risk of a vulnerable joint. Unwarranted mechanical stress can cause commencing malalignment, muscle failing, obesity and earlier joint grievance that distorted the structural reliability of the joint. In the perspective of this section, it is vital to note that a number of these risk factors for OA can be tailored through suitable lifestyle alterations.

CAUSES

Osteoarthritis

The majority of familiar kind of arthritis, ostecarthritis comprises wear and tear spoil to joint's cartilage, the hard, slick coating on the ends of bones. Enough damage can result in bone grinding directly on bone, which causes pain and restricted movement. This wear and tear can occur over many years, or it can be hastened by a joint injury or infection.

Rheumatoid Arthritis

In this type of arthritis, the body's immune co-ordination attacks the inside layer of the joint capsule, a tough membrane which covers all joint parts. This inside layer, recognized as the synovial membrane, alter in inflamed and swollen. The disease progression can sooner or later devastate cartilage and bone surrounded by the joint.

Management of Arthritis

The objective of treatment is to offer pain relief, boost joint mobility plus strength, and manage the disease to the degree that it is achievable. Treatment choices consist of medication; work out, heat/cold compresses, apply of joint security, and surgery. The treatment chart may engage combination of more than one of the options.

Arthritis View: With early verdict, the majority of arthritis types can be managed as well as the pain and disability reduced. In addition, early diagnosis with treatment may be capable to avoid tissue harm caused by arthritis. Early, forceful treatment is predominantly vital for rheumatoid arthritis in order to help to avoid added damage and disability downward the road.

Arthritis Anticipation: Although it may not be achievable to avert arthritis, there are ladder to take to diminish your risk of mounting the disease and to sluggish or prevent everlasting joint damage. These include:

(a) Maintenance of a healthy weight, surplus weight build strain on our joints.

(b) Keeping our muscles tough can help to protect and sustain the joints.

(c) Using joint protecting plans or support at workplace. Proper lifting and posture can help to protect your muscles and joints.

(d) A well balanced, nutritious diet can help to strengthen your bones and muscles.

IMPORTANCE OF LIFESTYLE

Medical experts agree that those living with rheumatoid arthritis should make certain lifestyle changes in order to limit the damage the disease can inflict on the body.

Like the treatments and cures, whether or not these lifestyle changes will definitively help is not yet certain. However, doctors suggest:

Quit smoking: According to Dr. Edward Skol, a rheumatologist with Scripps Health, environmental factors such as smoking can sometimes trigger the development of rheumatoid arthritis.

Use dietary supplements: Fish oils and omega-3a can help to control the inflammatory process of the disease, said Dr. Gregg Middleton, an associate clinical professor of rheumatology and orthopedics at the University of California, San Diego.

Lose weight: Dr. Natasha Conley, director of osteopathy at Kaiser Permanente, said it is common sense that less pressure on the weight bearing joints will ease discomfort for those with rheumatoid arthritis.

Perform low-impact exercises: Swimming, yoga, aerobics and other exercises that are easy on the joints can help to keep the body properly stretched while not placing too much pressure on the body, said Skol.

Follow an anti-inflammatory diet: "A healthy diet is a good thing, even though the relationship between specific foods (and rheumatoid arthritis) are not linked," Conley said. She stated that such foods would include fruits, vegetables and fish.

DO'S AND DON'TS OF LIFESTYLE IN MANAGEMENT OF ARTHRITIS
Do's
- Do strengthen your muscles.
- Do work with your rheumatologist.
- Do protect yourself with the proper gear.

Don'ts
- Don't smoke: RA is probably caused by a combination of the genes you are born with and certain events in your life that trigger those genes to become active. One of those triggers may be smoking.

- Don't drink alcohol if you are taking RA medications before checking with your doctor. Although moderate drinking may have some health benefits for people with RA, certain RA medications do not mix well with alcohol. These include the common RA drug methotrexate and non-steroidal anti-inflammatory drugs (NSAIDs).

- Don't spend all your time indoors. Getting about 15 minutes of sun exposure several days a week can help you get the vitamin D you need. Your skin uses the sun's rays to produce vitamin D. Studies show that vitamin D is important for your immune system and may help to prevent or relieve symptoms of RA. You also need vitamin D to absorb calcium, important for keeping your bones healthy. Supplements are another option for getting your vitamin D (without increasing your risk of skin cancer).

- Don't fall for any special diets that claim to cure RA. The best diet is well balanced and based on fruits, vegetables, and whole grains, with some healthy unsaturated (not saturated) fat. Radical diets that claim to cure RA or dramatically reduce your symptoms probably would not work and could be dangerous.

- Don't take fish oil supplements before checking with your doctor. There is some evidence that the omega-3 fatty acids found in cold water fish may be good for people with RA. Eating fish is fine, but taking high doses of supplements could interfere with several common medications and cause dangerous side effects.

Chapter 7

CANCER

We may never understand illnesses such as cancer. In fact, we may never cure it. But an ounce of prevention is worth more than a million pounds of cure.

— David Agus

INTRODUCTION

Cancer is a cluster of diseases relating abnormal cell growth by the potential to assault or extend to other part of body. It is also called as a malignant tumor, not every tumors are cancerous; benign tumors do not extend to other part. There are over 100 diverse known cancers that influence humans. Cancer is a multifaceted disease concerning numerous tempospatial alterations in cell physiology, that eventually escort to malignant tumors. Abnormal cell augmentation (neoplasia) is the natural endpoint of this disease. Tumor cell intrusion to adjacent tissues and far-off organs is the prime cause of morbidity and mortality for the majority of cancer patients. The biological course by which average cells are changed into malignant cancer cells have been the focus of a large study endeavor in the biomedical sciences for several decades. Regardless of this effort, cures or long-term managing strategies for metastatic cancer are as not easy today as they were 40 years since when President Richard Nixon stated a war on cancer.

The quarrel surrounds the starting point of cancer, contradictions and paradoxes have overwhelmed the field. Without an understandable idea on cancer genesis, it becomes tricky to devise a clear policy for efficient management. Although very precise processes lie beneath malignant makeover, a large quantity of non-specific influences can begin the disease together with radiation, chemicals, viruses, inflammation, etc. Indeed, it appears that prolonged exposure to almost any provocative agent in the surroundings can potentially origin cancer. That an incredibly specific course could be initiated in extremely unspecific way, considered "the oncogenic paradox". This paradox has remained largely unresolved.

In a milestone review, *Hanahan and Weinberg* recommended that six necessary alterations in cell physiology could trigger malignant cell growth. These six alterations were described as the hallmarks of almost all cancers are as follows:

1) Self-sufficiency in growth signals.
2) Insensitivity to growth inhibitory (antigrowth) signals.
3) Apoptosis (Evasion of programmed cell death).

4) Limitless replicative potential.

5) Angiogenesis (Sustained vascularity).

6) Tissue invasion and metastasis.

Genome instability, leading to increased mutability, was measured the crucial enabling trait for manifest the six hallmarks. However, the mutation speed for the majority genes is low, making it doubtful that the plentiful pathogenic mutations establish in cancer cells would take place intermittently within a regular human lifetime. This afterward shaped another paradox. If mutations are such uncommon actions, then how is it promising that cancer cells articulate so many diverse types and kinds of mutations?

The loss of genomic "caretakers" or else "guardians", concerned in sensing in addition to repairing DNA damage, was projected to explain the improved mutability of tumor cells. The defeat of this caretaker system would permit genomic volatility thus enabling pre-malignant cells to arrive at essential hallmarks of cancer. It has been difficult, however, to define with certainty the origin of pre-malignancy and the mechanisms by which the caretaker/guardian systems themselves are lost throughout the evolving malignant state. In accumulation to the six familiar hallmarks of cancer, aerobic glycolysis or the Warburg effect is also a vigorous metabolic hallmark of most tumors.

Substantiation is reviewed behind a general theory that cancer is chiefly an illness of energy metabolism. All of the key hallmarks of the disease can be associated to impair mitochondrial role. In order to uphold viability, tumor cells steadily shift to substrate level phosphorylation via glucose and glutamine as energy substrates. Whereas cancer causing germline mutations are unusual, the plenty of somatic genomic abnormalities originate in the mainstream of cancers can come up as a secondary effect of mitochondrial dysfunction. Systemic metastasis is the expected outcome subsequent lingering mitochondrial damage to cells of myeloid beginring. Tumor cells of myeloid source would obviously embody the competence to exit and go in tissues. Two chief conclusions come into view from the hypothesis; first that numerous cancers can revert if energy ingestion is limited and, second, that various cancers can be prohibited if energy intake is constrained. So, energy controlled diets united with drugs targeting glucose and glutamine can offer a rational approach for the longer-term managing and anticipation of most cancers.

Prevalence

Cancer is a foremost cause of death universally, measuring for 8.2 million deaths in 2012. The varying degree of most common causes of cancer death in cancers, for example: oesophageal cancer (400000 deaths), breast cancer (521000 deaths), colorectal cancer (694000 deaths), stomach (723000 deaths), liver cancer (745000 deaths), lung cancer (1.59 million deaths) etc.

India is expected to have more than 17.3 lakh new cases and over 8.8 lakh deaths due to the cancer by 2020 with different types e.g. breast, lung and cervix topping the list. In its projection, the ICMR (Indian Council of Medical Research) believed in 2020 the total number of new cancer cases is expected to be around nearly 17.3 lakh. Over 8.8 lakh patient are estimated to succumb by 2020. Data also exposed that only 12.5% of patients approach for treatment in the early hours of the disease. Breast cancer topped the list among females and mouth cancer among males. The northeast recorded highest cancer number equally in males and females. According to findings Aizawl district in Mizoram having the highest number of males cases while Papumpare district in Arunachal Pradesh recorded the highest number of cancer cases among females. Among males, present a noteworthy increase in the cases of cancers of colon, rectum and prostate in Bengaluru, Chennai and Delhi was observed. While among women there was a significant increase in the rate of cancers related to breast, uterus, ovary and lung. However, the PBCRs in Bangalore, Chennai, Barshi, Bhopal, Delhi and Mumbai have revealed a decrease in incident of cervical cancer. Delhi also tops chart for cancer amongst children.

SIGNS AND SYMPTOMS

- Changes in bowel or bladder habits
- Sore that does not cure.
- Curious bleeding or discharge.
- Lumps or thicken area in the breast, testicles, or someplace.
- Indigestion or trouble in swallowing.
- Change in the colour, size, shape, or thickness of a lump, mole, or mouth sore.
- Hoarseness or Cough which does not go off.

The following symptoms may also indication some cancer:

- Constant headaches
- Mysterious loss of weight or hunger.
- Persistent pain in bones or any new areas of the body.
- Constant fatigue, vomiting, or nausea.
- Determined low-grade fever, either steady or irregular.
- Repeated infection.

WHAT CAUSES CANCER?

Cancer initiate from one single cell. The conversion from a normal cell to tumour cell is a multistage process, typically a progression from a pre-cancerous lesion to malignant tumours.

These alterations are the outcome of the interaction among a person's genetic factor and three categories of outer agents, including:

- Physical carcinogens, like ultraviolet and ionizing radiation.
- Chemical carcinogens, e.g. asbestos, components of tobacco burn, a food contaminant like aflatoxin and / or a drinking water contaminant e.g. arsenic.
- Biological carcinogens, such as infections as of certain viruses, bacteria or parasites.

Through its cancer research agency i.e. International Agency for Research on Cancer (IARC), WHO keeps a categorization of cancer causing agents.

Ageing is one more basic factor for the progress of cancer, the rate of cancer rise noticeably with age, most likely owing to a assemble up of risks for precise cancers that raise with age. The overall risk accrual is united with the tendency for cellular repair mechanisms to be less effective as a person grows older.

Risk Factors for Cancers

Use of tobacco, habitual alcohol drinking, physical inactivity and unhealthy diet are the main risk factors of cancer worldwide. In low- and middle-income countries several chronic infections have major relevance and are risk factors for cancer. Hepatitis B (HBV), hepatitis C virus (HCV) along with various types of human papilloma virus (HPV) increases the threat for liver and cervical cancer correspondingly. Infection with HIV significantly increases the risk of cancer such as cervical cancer.

Understanding about the cause of cancer, and interventions to avert and handle the disease is far-reaching. Cancer can be condensed and inhibited by implementing evidence-based strategies for prevention of cancer, early detection and management of patients through cancer. Numerous cancers have a high possibility of cure if detected before time and treated effectively.

Modifying and Avoiding Risk Factors

By modifying key risk factors more than 30% of cancer deaths may perhaps be prevented, that mainly includes: Tobacco use, lack of physical activity, use of alcohol, low fruit and vegetable intake with unhealthy diet, HPV-infection transmitted sexually, infection by HBV, being overweight or obese, ionizing and non-ionizing radiation, urban air pollution, indoor smoke from household use of solid fuels.

Globally, use of tobacco is the single most significant risk factor for cancer causing about 20% of cancer deaths and around 70% of lung cancer deaths. In many low-income countries, up to 20% of cancer deaths are owing to infection by HBV and HPV.

Avoidance strategies may include a due care of raise awareness about prevention of the risk factors as listed above.

- Vaccinate against human papilloma virus (HPV) and hepatitis B virus (HBV).
- Occupational hazards control.
- Decrease contact to non-ionizing radiation by sunlight (UV).
- Decrease exposure to ionizing radiation (occupational or medical diagnostic imaging).

COMMON MYTHS AND MISUNDERSTANDINGS

- All cancers are the same.
- There is no cure.
- Cell phones cause cancer.
- Any lumps or large masses detected during cancer screenings are cancerous.
- Artificial sweeteners cause cancer.
- All you need to beat cancer is a positive attitude, not treatment.
- Surgery could cause cancer to spread throughout the body.
- Only women get breast cancer.
- The prevalence of cancer is on the rise.
- Medical science already has and is withholding a cure for cancer.

CAUSES OF CANCER

Chemicals: Particular substances have been linked to specific types of cancer. Tobacco smoking is associated with many forms of cancer, and causes 90% of lung cancer. Daily long term vaping with a high voltage (5.0 V) electronic cigarette may generate formaldehyde forming chemicals at a larger intensity than smoking, which was dogged to be a lifetime cancer risk of around 5 to 15 times greater as compare to smoking.

Many mutagens are also carcinogens, but some carcinogens are not mutagens. Alcohol is an example of a chemical carcinogen that is not a mutagen. In Western Europe, 10% of males and 3% of females are attributed to alcohol induced cancers.

A verified the link among tobacco use and incidences of cancer in the lung, larynx, head, neck, stomach, bladder, kidney, oesophagus and pancreas. Tobacco smokes consist of over fifty identified carcinogens, counting nitrosamines and polycyclic aromatic hydrocarbons. Tobacco is accountable for regarding one in three of all cancer deaths in the developed world, and as regards one in five worldwide. However, the figures of smokers are still rising globally, leading to what now have described as the tobacco endemic.

Cancer associated to one's occupation is said to represent involving 2–20% of all cases. Every year, at least 200,000 citizens die worldwide due to cancer related to their workplace. Most cancer deaths caused by occupational risk factors occur in the developed world. Millions of employees run the danger of developing cancers such as lung cancer and mesothelioma from inhaling asbestos fibre and tobacco smoke, or leukemia from contact to benzene at their work places.

Diet and Exercise: Diet, physical inactivity, and obesity are related to roughly 30–35% of cancer deaths. In the United States, excess body weight is related with the development of various types of cancer and is a factor in range of 14–20% of all cancer deaths. Physical inactivity is supposed to give to cancer risk not only through its consequence on body weight but also during negative effects on immune and endocrine system. Over half of the effect commencing diet is due to excess of nutrition rather than from eating too little healthy foods.

Diets which are low in vegetables, fruits plus whole grains and high in processed or red meats are connected with a variety of cancers. A high-salt diet is related to gastric cancer, aflatoxin B1, a repeated food contamination, with liver cancer, and Betel nut chewing [Supari and related product] among oral cancer. This may partly clarify differences in cancer occurrence in different countries. For instance, gastric cancer is regular in Japan due to its high-salt diet and colon cancer is more frequent in the United States. Immigrants build-up the risk of their new country, often in one generation, signifying a substantial relationship between diet and cancer.

Infection: Worldwide around 18% of cancer deaths are connected to infectious diseases. These percentages vary in diverse regions of the world from as high of 25% in Africa to less than 10% in the industrial world. Viruses are the customary infectious agents that cause cancer but bacteria and parasites may as well have an effect.

An oncovirus is virus that can cause cancer. These comprise human papillomavirus (cervical carcinoma), Epstein Barr virus (B-cell lymphoproliferative disease and nasopharyngeal carcinoma), Kaposi's sarcoma herpes virus (Kaposi's sarcoma and primary effusion lymphomas), hepatitis B and hepatitis C viruses (hepatocellular carcinoma), and Human T-cell leukemia virus-1 (T-cell leukemias). Bacterial infection may also increase the risk of cancer, as noticed in *H. pylori* induced gastric carcinoma. Parasitic infections powerfully related with cancer include *Schistosoma haematobium* (squamous cell carcinoma of the bladder) and the liver flukes, *Opisthorchis* viverrini and *Clonorchis sinensis* (cholangiocarcinoma).

Radiation: Up to 10% of invasive cancers are associated to radiation disclosure, together with both ionizing radiation and non-ionizing ultraviolet radiation. Furthermore, the enormous majority of non-invasive cancers are non-melanoma skin cancers occurred due to non-ionizing ultraviolet radiation.

Sources of ionizing radiation comprise medical imaging, as well as radon gas. Radiation can act as a source of cancer in most parts of the body, in all animals, and at any age, while radiation induced solid tumors typically take 10–15 years, and can take up to 40 years, to become clinically evident, and radiation induced leukemias characteristically require 2–10 years to become noticeable. Some people, like those with nevoid basal cell carcinoma syndrome or retinoblastoma, are more vulnerable than usual to develop cancer from radiation exposure. Children and adolescents are twice as expected to expand radiation induced leukemia as adults; radiation exposure prior to birth has ten times the consequence. Ionizing radiation is not a predominantly strong mutagen. Residential contact to radon gas, for instance, has comparable cancer risks as passive smoking. Low-dose exposures, such as living near a nuclear power plant, are normally supposed to have no or very little result on cancer improvement. Radiation is a more potent cause of cancer when it is united with additional cancer causing agents, such as radon gas exposure and smoking tobacco.

Contrasting chemical or physical triggers for cancer, ionizing radiation hits molecules inside cells indiscriminately. If it happens to strike a chromosome, it can rupture the chromosome, result in an abnormal quantity of chromosomes, and inactivate one or more genes in the part of the chromosome that it hit, delete parts of the DNA sequence, cause chromosome translocations, or cause other types of chromosome abnormalities. Most important damage usually fallout in the cell dying, but slighter damage may leave a steady, partly functional cell that may be competent of proliferating and mounting into cancer, particularly if tumor suppressor genes were damaged by the radiation. Three autonomous stages come into view to be concerned in the formation of cancer with ionizing radiation: morphological alterations in the cell, adopting cellular immortality (losing normal, life-limiting cell regulatory processes), and adaptations that support formation of a tumor. Even if the radiation particle does not strike the DNA straight, it triggers response from cells that indirectly boost the likelihood of mutations.

Wide variety of medical application of ionizing radiation is a mounting source of radiation induced cancers. Ionizing radiation may be used to treat other cancers, but this may, in few instances, induce a second form of cancer. It is as well used in some kinds of medical imaging. It is expected that 0.4% of cancers in 2007, in the United States are because of CTs performed in the past and that this may enhance to as high as 1.5–2% with rates of CT usage throughout same time era.

Prolonged exposure to ultraviolet radiation from the solar rays can direct to melanoma and other skin malignancies. Clear confirmation establishes ultraviolet radiation, particularly the non-ionizing medium wave UVB, as the reason of most non-melanoma skin cancers that are the most frequent types of cancer in the world. Non-ionizing radio frequency radiations from mobile phones, electric power transmission, and other similar sources have been described as a possible carcinogen by the World Health Organization's International Agency for Research on Cancer. Though, studies have not found a reliable link between cell phone radiation and cancer risk.

Heredity: The enormous majority of cancers are non-hereditary ("sporadic cancers"). Hereditary cancers are first and foremost caused by an inherited genetic imperfection. Less than 0.3% of the populations are carriers of a genetic mutation which has a large consequence on cancer risk and this cause less than 3–10% of all cancer. Some of these syndromes comprises: certain inherited mutations within the genes BRCA1 and BRCA2 through a more than 75% risk of breast cancer and ovarian cancer, and Hereditary Non-polyposis Colorectal Cancer (HNPCC or Lynch syndrome) which is there in about 3% of people with colorectal cancer, surrounded by others.

Physical Agents: Some substances forms foundation of cancer principally through their physical, rather than chemical, effects on cells. A prominent example of this is extended exposure to asbestos; naturally happening mineral fibres which are a major cause of mesothelioma, which is a cancer of the serous membrane, usually the serous membrane adjacent the lungs. Additional substances in this category, counting both naturally occurring and synthetic asbestos like fibres such as wollastonite, attapulgite, glass wool, and rock wool, are assumed to have comparable effects. Non-fibrous particulate materials to cause cancer embrace powdered metallic cobalt and nickel, and crystalline silica (quartz, cristobalite, and tridymite). Regularly, physical carcinogens must get within the body (for instance when inhaling tiny pieces) and needs years of exposure to build-up cancer.

Physical trauma converting into cancer is fairly exceptional, claims that breaking bones resulted in bone cancer, for instance, have never been confirmed. Correspondingly, physical trauma is not accepted as grounds for cervical cancer, breast cancer, or brain cancer. One conventional source is common, long-term application of hot matter to the body. It is likely that frequent burns on the similar part of the body, such as those produced by kairo heaters (charcoal hand warmers), may lead to skin cancer, in particular if carcinogenic chemicals are also present. Often drinking steaming hot tea may turn out esophageal cancer, normally, it is assumed that the cancer arises, or a pre-existing cancer is encouraged, during the process of repair, fairly than the cancer being caused directly by the trauma. However, frequent injuries to the same tissues may endorse unwarranted cell proliferation that could boost the odds of a cancerous mutation. There is no confirmation that inflammation itself causes cancer, yet inflammation can add to proliferation, survival and migration of cancer cells by influencing the microenvironment around tumors.

Hormones: Some of the hormones play a role in the progress of cancer by promoting cell propagation. Insulin-like growth factors and their required proteins play a key responsibility in cancer cell propagation, separation and apoptosis, signifying possible association in carcinogenesis. Hormones are important agents in sex related cancers for instance cancer of the breast, endometrium, prostate, thyroid cancer, ovary or testis, and bone cancer. For example, the daughters of women having breast cancer have notably higher levels of estrogen as well as progesterone than the daughters of women without breast cancer. These elevated hormone levels may clarify why such women have higher risk of breast cancer, even in the deficiency of a breast cancer gene. Correspondingly, men of African lineage have significantly elevated levels of testosterone than men of European ancestry, and have a correspondingly much higher level of prostate tumor. Men of Asian heritage, with the lowest levels of testosterone activating androstanediol glucuronide, contain the lowest levels of prostate cancer.

Other factors are also related, obese people have higher levels of some hormones allied with cancer and a higher rate of that types of cancers. Women who take hormone replacement therapy have a comparatively higher risk of developing cancers related to those hormones. Alternatively, people who exercise far more than average have lower levels of such hormones, and decreased risk of cancer. Osteosarcoma might be promoted by growth hormones, some treatments and prevention approaches influence this cause by artificially dropping hormone levels, and thus discourage hormone sensitive cancers.

Apart from these exceptional transmissions that happen with pregnancies and only a subsidiary few organ donors, cancer is by and large not a transmissible disease. The main reason for this is tissue graft rejection cause by MHC incompatibility. Humans and other vertebrates, the immune system uses MHC antigens to differentiate between "self" and "non-self" cells because these antigens are different from person to person. When non-self antigens are encountered, the immune system reacts against the appropriate cell. Such reactions may guard against tumor cell engraftment by eliminating implanted cells. In the United States, approximately 3,500 pregnant women have a malignancy per annum, in addition to transplacental transmission of acute leukemia, lymphoma, melanoma along with carcinoma from mother to fetus has been observed. The development of donor derived tumors from organ transplants is remarkably exceptional. The chief grounds of organ transplant related tumors appear to be malignant melanoma, which was hidden at the time of organ harvest. Job stress does not come into sight to be a noteworthy factor at least in lung, colorectal, breast in addition to prostate cancers.

MANAGEMENT

For cancer treatment various options are present, the primary ones together with surgery, chemotherapy, radiation, hormonal therapy, targeted and palliative care. These treatments are used depends on the category, location, and grade of the cancer in addition to the person's health. The treatment intent may be curative or non-curative.

CHEMOTHERAPY

It is the treatment of cancer by one or more cytotoxic anti-neoplastic drugs (chemotherapeutic agents) as part of a standardized course of therapy. The term encompasses any of a large range of different anticancer drugs that are divided into wide categories for instance alkylating agents and antimetabolites. Traditional chemotherapeutic agents act by killing cells that divide rapidly, one of the main properties of most cancer cells.

Targeted therapy is a variety of chemotherapy which targets precise molecular differences among cancer cells and normal cells. The first targeted therapy to be developed blocked the estrogen receptor molecule, inhibiting the growth of breast cancer. Another frequent example is the class of Bcr-Abl inhibitors, which are used to treat Chronic Myelogenous Leukemia [CML]. At present, there are targeted therapies for breast cancer, multiple myeloma, lymphoma, prostate cancer, melanoma etc.

The efficacy of chemotherapy depends on the type of cancer and the stage. In association with surgery, chemotherapy has proven helpful in a number of different cancer types including: breast cancer, colorectal cancer, pancreatic cancer, osteogenic sarcoma, testicular cancer, ovarian cancer, and certain lung cancers. The overall effectiveness ranges from being curative for some cancers, such as some leukemias, to being ineffective, such as in some brain tumors, to being needless in others, like most non-melanoma skin cancers. The effectiveness of chemotherapy is often limited by toxicity to other tissues in the body. Even when it is impracticable for chemotherapy to recommend a permanent cure, chemotherapy may be useful to reduce symptoms like pain or to reduce the size of a deadly tumor in the hope that surgery will be possible in the future.

Radiation

This therapy involves the use of ionizing radiation in an attempt to either cure or improve the symptoms of cancer. It works by damaging the DNA of cancerous tissue causing cellular death. To spare normal tissues (like skin or organs), a specially shaped radiation beams are targeted from numerous angles of contact to intersect at the tumor, providing a much larger absorbed dose than surrounding, healthy tissue. As with chemotherapy, different cancers respond differently to radiation therapy.

Radiation therapy is used in around half of all cases and can be from either internal sources in the form of brachytherapy or external radiation source. The radiation is most usually low energy X-rays for treating skin cancers while higher energy X-ray beams are used in the treatment of cancers within the body. Radiation is usually used in addition to surgery and/or chemotherapy but for certain types of cancer, such as early head and neck cancer, may be used alone. For painful bone metastasis, it has been found to be effective in about 70% of people.

Surgery

It is a primary method of treatment of the majority isolated solid cancers and may play a role in palliation and prolongation of survival. It is typically a vital part of making the ultimate diagnosis and staging the tumor as biopsies are frequently necessary. In localized cancer surgery classically attempt to remove the whole mass together with, in certain cases, the lymph nodes in the area. For some types of cancer this is all that is desirable to get rid of the cancer.

Palliative Care

This refers to healing that attempts to make the person feel better and may or may not be combined with an effort to treat the cancer. Palliative cares include action to reduce the physical, emotional, spiritual, and psycho-social distress experienced by patient. Contrasting treatment that is intended at directly killing cancer cells, the main objective of palliative care is to advance the person's quality of life.

People at all stages of cancer treatment should encompass some manner of palliative care to offer comfort. In some cases, medical specialty professional organizations advise that people and physicians react to cancer only with palliative care and not with cure directed therapy. This includes:

- People with low performance status, matching with limited capability to care for themselves.
- People who established no advantage from prior evidence based treatments.
- People who are not appropriate to join in any suitable clinical trial.
- People for whom the physician sees no strong proof that treatment would be effective.

It is often mystified with hospice and therefore only involved when people move toward end of life. Like hospice care, palliative care attempts to help the person cope with the instant requirements and to augment the person's comfort. Unlike hospice care, palliative care does not need people to prevent treatment aimed at prolonging their lives or curative the cancer.

Multiple national medical strategy suggest early palliative care for people whose cancer has created distressing symptoms (pain, shortness of breath, fatigue, nausea) or who need help coping with their illness. In people who have metastatic disease when first diagnosed, oncologists should consider a palliative care consult instantly. Furthermore, an oncologist should believe a palliative care confer with in any person they feel has less than 12 months of life even if ongoing aggressive treatment.

Immunotherapy

A variety of therapies using immunotherapy, stimulating or helping the immune system to fight cancer, have come into use since 1997, and this continues to be an area of very active research.

Alternative Medicine

Complementary and alternative cancer treatments are a assorted group of healthcare systems, practices, and products that are not part of conventional medicine. "Complementary medicine" refers to methods and substances used along with conventional medicine, while "alternative medicine" refers to compounds used instead of conventional medicine. Most complementary and alternative medicines for cancer have not been rigorously studied or tested. Some alternative treatments have been investigated and shown to be ineffective but still continue to be marketed and promoted.

LIFESTYLE AND CANCER

Physical Activity and Cancer Prevention

The mainly believable confirmation for the profit of physical activity on cancer avoidance exists for colon and breast cancer. Moderate to vigorous aerobic, for 30 to 60 minutes a day, reduces the risk of colon cancer by around 30%. There appear to be a dose response relationship with increasing activity associated with reducing risk. The mechanisms accountable for the involvement of physical activity and colon cancer have not all been elucidated, but it has been suggested that physical activity may reduce body fat and increase insulin sensitivity. Other possible mechanisms may relate to improved immune function and decrease gut transit time which reduces exposure to carcinogens.

More than two dozen cohort studies along with even a greater number of population based studies have establish that physically active women have a lesser risk of developing breast cancer compared to sedentary women. In general, there is convincing substantiation that moderate and high levels of physical activity are linked with a 20% to 40% reduction in the danger of breast cancer. The effects appear to be clearer in postmenopausal contrast to premenopausal women. There are numerous mechanisms whereby physical activity may protect against breast cancer. These includes the reduction in oestrogen and androgen concentration, amplification of immune function and decrease in body fat. Furthermore, there is accumulating evidence that physically active individuals have a condensed danger of lung, endometrial, prostate and ovarian cancers compare to sedentary peoples.

Thus, as in the case of most of the non-communicable chronic diseases described in this series, the usual advice is that all adults do reasonably intense cardiorespiratory exercise for 30 minutes a day, five days per week or vigorously intense cardiorespiratory exercise for 20 minutes/day, three days/week. In addition all adults should do 8 to 10 strength training exercises, 8 to 12 repetitions of each exercise twice/week.

The Role of Physical Exercise and Cancer Management

Until fairly in recent times it was thought that as a patient was diagnosed with cancer, they should undertake rest and avoid physical activity, specifically if the patient was to agree to intervention including surgery, chemotherapy or else radiation therapy. However, an increasing number of studies have investigated the effects of exercise training in primary cancer treatment and after cancer treatments have been done. At the same time as the majority have documented influence of physical exercise in patients with breast cancer and colon cancer, very few studies have investigated the effects of physical work out on patients with other cancers. The literature consistently indicates that exercise training throughout cancer treatment is safe and sound, as well as has positive effects on cardiorespiratory health, quality of life, and maintenance of skeletal muscle mass and reduces side effects of cancer treatment.

Besides cancer survivors are at augmented risk for co-morbid circumstances counting cardiovascular disease, diabetes, osteoporosis, obesity, and hypertension which may be due to genetic inclination, lifestyle or cancer treatment consideration. However, there is clear payback for persistence of exercise following treatment, particularly with respect to reappearance, cancer specific mortality and all reasons of death in cancer survivors.

The physiological profits of exercise education during and after treatment includes:

- Enhanced joint range of motion, increase in muscle strength, stamina and ability.
- Better quality of life, self esteem enhanced fitness, mood along with functional capacity with respect to activities of daily living.
- Modest decline of fatigue, better body image as well as sense of control.
- Reduced body fat, increased skeletal muscle strength and improved body composition.
- Increased chemotherapy completion rates.
- Reduced nausea and other treatment related side effects.
- Favorable changes in concentrations of androgens, oestrogens, growth factors (IGF-I and IGFBP-3), adipokines (leptin and adiponectin) and markers of inflammation (u-CRP).
- Participation in 3 hours/week of moderate intensity exercise after diagnosis of colon cancer is associated with a significant reduction in the risk of colon cancer death and reduction in risk of total death compared with patients with colon cancer who do not exercise.

Yet, it is estimated that only a few colorectal cancer survivors and breast cancer survivors participate in standard physical exercise during treatment. This might be due to the fact that there has been a lack of prioritization of lifestyle associated factors in patient management in the healthcare structure. Certainly, family practitioners and oncologists might not have been aware of the benefits of physical exercise in this patient group. On top, non-availability of medical aid cover for supervised exercise rehabilitation or lifestyle counseling, lack of adequate facilities or the confusion of patients on whether physical activity might pick up their clinical result might be contributing factor.

Useful considerations in prescribing work-out for the secondary prevention of chronic cardiovascular disease

Few patients with cancer may prefer to exercise alone otherwise a number of might like a group. It is however important that each patient is individually assessed prior to exercise by a professional expert in work out therapy. As each patient is inclined by the nature of the particular cancer or tumor, stage of disease, and effects of the various forms of treatments, exercise prescription requires wide individualization. Strategies to overcome barriers to increase physical inactivity and promote compliance with healthy eating and exercise interventions need to be well review.

The effects of the various treatment options for patients with cancer need to be carefully considered. Many of the therapies may reduce the patient's ability for physical action owing to adverse effects on the cardiopulmonary, neurological or else musculoskeletal system. Thus, a cardiovascular assessment for patients embarking on an exercise agenda is significant. So, each patient should be evaluated briefly prior to every exercise short time as an acute change in state might form a contraindication to exercise.

Furthermore, patients are often in a debilitated state and be limited by pain. Exercise should therefore start at a very low intensity and duration and progression of the program should be very gradual, with constant re-evaluation.

Additionally clinical considerations in support of the exercising patient should comprise of:

- Avoidance of patients with indwelling catheters and access lines microbial exposure, and keep away from resistance training in the region of the catheter.
- In case the platelet count of patient falls below < 50000/mm^3, a danger of bleeding needs to be considered and exercise modified accordingly.
- Severe anemia (Hb < 10 g/dl) should alert the clinician to delay exercise, lower exercise intensity or consider an amplified possibility of cardiovascular complication through exercise.
- The person with peripheral neuropathy might have deficient balance and/or weakness. These patients might have greater benefit from stationary cycling compared to other forms of aerobic workout.

- The immune compromised patient should avoid public gyms until white cell counts return to normal.
- Patients undergoing   radiation therapy should avoid chlorine exposure to the irradiated skin.

Psychosocial Interventions

Cancer is a cruel and potentially life threatening disease that, possibly more than any other medical condition. It affects individual's psychological well-being, daily functioning and efficiency. The disease has a border of various complex dimensions like issues of mortality, managing side effects of medication, dealing with pain along with associated psychiatric morbidity, for example, anxiety and depression. The often pragmatic scientific come across in primary care in which the person with negligible ailments, when pressed, admit that deep down they fear they have cancer, lends receipt to the major subjective magnitude.

The role of psychosocial interventions in the management of cancer has been, and continues to be, extensively researched, with the most pressing question (certainly from the perspective of the patient) being whether these interventions significantly improve survival. How are primary care clinicians and indeed oncologists to interpret and utilize these data for the benefit of patients?

Three broad principals are worth consideration:

- Psychological self-regulation and limited emotional appearance may improve longevity in convinced patients. Group interventions are most cost-effective and would include health education, stress management, coping techniques and psychosocial group support. All of these interventions may be explored in individual therapy as well.
- Psychological self-regulation and emotional expressivity are more likely to enhance well-being irrespective of effect on survival rates.
- Management of associated co-morbidities, especially anxiety and depression, may enhance well-being and quality of life.

These broad principals, alongside clinical common sense and empathic attunement to the subjective experience of the patient, dealing with each patient on their own terms, will at the very least, reduce suffering and anguish in what is always a psychologically challenging and life altering experience and offers the hope of extending survival in certain patients, though unpredictably.

Dietary Intervention

Once a patient has been diagnosed with cancer, eating well becomes increasingly important during management. Selecting the correct foods not only assists the body in potentially fighting the disease, but could also ease the side effects of medical treatment regimens. Once cancer has been successfully treated, a well-selected diet could lower the risk of recurrence. Early dietary intervention is essential as cancer and nutrition interact in two ways:

1. Nutrition can affect cancer at every stage, changing tumor growth and assisting immunity. In this sense, it is important to consume those foods with maximum immune enhancing potential.

2. Cancer can affect a patient's nutritional status. The mere stress of being diagnosed with the disease can disrupt healthy eating habits. Furthermore, both the cancer and its various therapies could deplete the body of vital nutrients, subsequently leading to weight loss or weight gain, each of which could impair the body's immune system.

General Dietary Considerations

The general dietary guidelines that are advised to a patient diagnosed with cancer are as follows:

*   **Adequate Protein Intake:** During times of stress and illness the body generally requires more protein. In addition to this, adequate protein is required to assist in the repair and building of tissues affected by cancer therapy, as well as to support the immune system. Adequate amounts of protein should thus be consumed during all stages of treatment and recovery. Very high protein diets are however not suggested. To ensure the intake of adequate protein, it is advised that protein sources low in saturated fats, such as fish, lean skinless poultry, eggs, fat trimmed lean cuts of meat, low fat and fat free dairy products, nuts, seeds and legumes, are selected. For specific protein requirements, it is advised that a person seeks the assistance of a registered dietitian.

*   **Wholegrain Carbohydrates:** Whole grain foods, as well as fruit and vegetables are the best recommended sources of carbohydrate as they are rich in essential nutrients, phytochemicals and fibre. It is advised that these foods should make up the majority of an individual's dietary intake, whilst simultaneously, minimizing the intake of refined foods such as white bread, and the like, and products with added sugar, which are energy dense and not substantial contributors of essential nutrients.

*   **The Role of Dietary Fat:** It is advised that fatty cuts of meats (such as sausages and bacon) be avoided, and that the skin of chicken be removed. Furthermore, fat needs to be trimmed off meat before cooking. Advise patients to opt for low fat or fat free dairy products (unless the aim is specifically to gain weight and/or if the patient is experiencing cachexia). Further advice should include the avoidance of fried foods and commercially baked goods such as pies, pastries and muffins. The type of fat in the

diet is also important. Healthier (unsaturated) fats are found in olive oil, canola oil, avocado, nuts and seeds. Also advise the consumption of foods rich in omega 3 fatty acids, such as fatty fish (e.g. salmon, sardines and mackerel).

- **Vegetables and Fruits:** The diet should include a variety of fruits and vegetables of different colours, textures and flavours. The recommendation is to aim for at least five to nine or more servings daily, as this will ensure the intake of a wide range of different vitamins, minerals and other micronutrients. Consuming adequate fruit and vegetables not only improves survival after cancer, but also reduces the risk that the cancer will recur. Cooked vegetables also contribute to the recommended daily intake.

  Though the cooking process might slightly reduce the vitamin content, it is also known to increase the absorption of many nutrients, and furthermore, decreases the risk for any food-borne infections. Peeling and cooking fruit and vegetables can further reduce the risk of acquiring a food-borne infection.

- **Hydration:** Six to eight glasses of fluids is the daily recommendation, in order to ensure that the patient's tissues are well hydrated.

- **Reduce Alcohol Intake:** Drinking alcohol in large amounts increases the risk of developing cancerous tumors in the breast and possibly also in the colon and rectum. Some investigation found that drinking of alcohol may also lead to cancers of the mouth, pharynx, larynx, oesophagus and liver. It is advised that alcohol intake should be limited to two drinks a day for men and one drink a day for women. Reducing alcohol intake can offer additional benefits in susceptible individuals.

- **Dietary Variety:** Throughout cancer treatment and recovery, it is advocated that a patient select from a wide range of different foods, to ensure the intake of all the necessary nutrients in adequate quantities. No single food contains all the required nutrients, hence, the consumption of a varied diet will ensure an overall better nutrient intake from the diet.

- **Commercial Dietary Supplements:** It is important to emphasize the fact that food is the best, and preferred, source of vitamins and minerals, and patients should aim to get all their nutrients by following a nutritious diet. Additional vitamin and mineral supplements should only be considered when difficulty experienced with dietary intake, particularly during treatment and recovery. However, high doses of certain vitamins and minerals could lead to potential side effects and could even increase the risk of developing certain cancers. In particular, it is important to avoid high doses of antioxidant supplements, such as vitamin A, C, E, beta carotene, zinc and selenium. Antioxidants support cellular repair, which means that in high doses (as from supplements), they might also promote the survival of cancer cells, and could potentially interfere with cancer therapy. Beta carotene supplements in high doses, for example, have been found to increase the risk of lung cancer.

It is considered safe to take multivitamin and mineral supplements at levels that do not exceed 100% of the recommended daily allowance (RDA). It is advised that a patient consult with their healthcare practitioner, such as a dietitian or doctor, before commencing the intake of any supplements.

- *Food Supplements:* Patients often experience difficulty in consuming adequate energy from food, often due to nausea or difficulty in swallowing. Liquid nutritional supplements could assist in providing the nutrients and energy needed to maintain weight/prevent weight loss, in this regard.

Commercial meal replacement supplements are available; however, patients could also try these home-made options:

- o   Fruit smoothies made by blending fresh fruits and yoghurts, or vegetable juices blended together, will assist in providing more vitamins and minerals.
- o   Juicing fruits and vegetables might also increase the absorption of certain nutrients.
- o   Soups can be made by liquidizing fresh vegetables and potatoes together with protein sources such as chicken, beans, lentils or chick peas, which can then be served with soft bread/bread rolls.
- o   Adding healthy fats to these self prepared dishes such as raw, unsalted nuts, olive or canola oil and avocado pear – can increase their health benefits and enable the patient to consume more kilojoules.

Weight Maintenance: The maintenance of a healthy body weight is important as both weight loss and weight gain could be detrimental to the patient. All nutrient stores are needed to best cope with any medical treatment regimen, particularly the potential side effects related thereto, as well as to assist in the recovery period. Unintentional weight loss should thus be combated by attempting to consume adequate protein, aimed at restoring body weight to its pre-cancer level. Suggest that patients increase their meal frequency, and to opt for energy-dense, high quality foods.

Conversely, being overweight increases the risk that cancer might recur. If the patient is overweight or obese, gradual weight loss is advised at a maximum of 0.5–1 kg a week. Ensure that the diet is nutritious and well balanced, and that their weight management program is approved by the oncologist and/or dietitian.

Smoking Cessation: Nearly one third of all cancers are caused by smoking, thus there is a high incidence of smokers amongst all patients with cancer. Smoking is associated with poor outcomes including progressive disease, second primaries and increased comorbidity. The general practitioner has a critical role to play in advising and assisting smokers to quit by integrating the various aspects of nicotine dependence.

Counseling and pharmacotheraeutic interventions for smoking cessation are among the most cost-effective clinical interventions.

This topic has provided outline of the basic lifestyle modifications to consider in the management of patients with cancer. A holistic view with respect to exercise training, dietary modification, psychosocial interventions and smoking cessation are all important in patient management. General practitioners and oncologists should particularly be aware of the benefits of exercise and healthy nutritional interventions and assist their patients by suggesting adherence to accepted physical activity and nutritional guidelines. All patients should therefore be afforded the time and interest of their general practitioner so that they may assist their patients in making well informed choices with respect to their lifestyle to promote health and manage disease.

Chapter 8

ALZEHEIMERS

"Alzheimer is the cleverest thief, because it not only steals from your identity, but it steals the very thing you need to remember what's been stolen."

— *Jarod Kintz*

INTRODUCTION

Alzheimer's disease (AD) is a persistent neuro degenerative illness which usually starts bit by bit and as time passes gets worse. The common early indication is trouble in remembering current events (short-term memory loss). As the sickness advances, symptoms can comprise troubles with language, confusion (easily getting lost), loss of motivation, mood swings, not managing self care, and behavioral issues due to brain architecture (Fig. 8.1). As a person's situation declines, they often remove from relations and society. Gradually, physical functions are vanished, eventually leading to death. Although the pace of development can vary, the normal life expectancy following diagnosis is three to nine years.

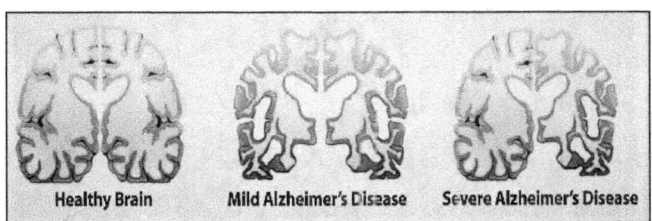

Fig. 8.1: Brain degeneration in Alzheimer's

No treatments prevent or reverse its development though some may temporarily improve symptoms. Affected people more and more depend on others for help, often placing an ever mounting burden on the caregiver. These pressures can include social, psychological, physical, and economic elements. Exercise programs are advantageous with esteem to behavior of daily living and can potentially press forward outcomes. Treatment of behavioral problems or psychosis due to dementia with antipsychotics is regular but not typically suggested due to little benefit and an increased risk of early death.

PREVALENCE

In 2010, there were between 21 and 35 million people worldwide with AD. It mainly begins in people over 65 years of age; while 4% to 5% of cases are early-onset Alzheimer's which begin before this. It affects around 6% of people 65 years and older. In 2010, dementia caused about 486,000 deaths. It was first introduced by, and afterward named subsequent to, German psychiatrist and pathologist Alois Alzheimer in 1906. In developed countries, AD is one of the most financially costly diseases.

There is an estimated 46.8 million people worldwide living with dementia in 2015. These numbers will almost double every 20 years, reaching 74.7 million up to 2030 and 131.5 million by 2050, most of the increase will be in developing countries. Already 58% of people with dementia live in developing countries, but by 2050 this will rise to 68%. The highest growth in the elderly population is captivating place in China, India, and their south Asian and western Pacific neighbours.

SIGNS AND SYMPTOMS OF ALZHEIMER'S

- Memory loss that disrupts daily life.
- Trouble in planning or solving problems.
- Difficulty in implementation of familiar tasks at home, at work or at leisure.
- Confusion with time or place.
- Trouble in understanding visual images moreover spatial relations.
- New-fangled problems with words in dialogue or lettering.
- Misplacing things and losing the ability to repeat steps.
- Decreased or reduced decision making.
- Pulling out from job or social actions.
- Changes in mood and personality.

COMMON MYTHS AND MISUNDERSTANDINGS ABOUT ALZHEIMER

- Alzheimer's happens only to older people.
- Alzheimer's symptoms are a normal part of aging.
- Alzheimer's doesn't lead to death.
- There are treatments that stop the disease from getting worse.
- Alzheimer's is caused by aluminium, flu shots, silver fillings, or aspartame.
- People with Alzheimer's become agitated, violent and aggressive.
- People with Alzheimer's cannot function, cannot have a quality of life, and cannot enjoy activities.

CAUSES

Even though the causes of Alzheimer's are not yet fully understood, its consequence on the brain is clear. It damage moreover kills brain cells. A brain exaggerated by AD has numerous fewer cells and many smaller quantity connections among existing cells than do a healthy brain (Fig: 8.2).

Plaques: These are clumps of a protein called beta-amyloid may damage and destroy brain cells in different ways, including intrusive with cell to cell communication. Though the ultimate cause of brain cell death in Alzheimer's is not known, the assortment of beta-amyloid on the outer surface of brain cells is a prime guess.

Tangles: Brain cells depend on an internal support and transport system to carry nutrients and other essential resources all the way through their long extensions. This system needs the normal structure as well as function of a protein known as tau.

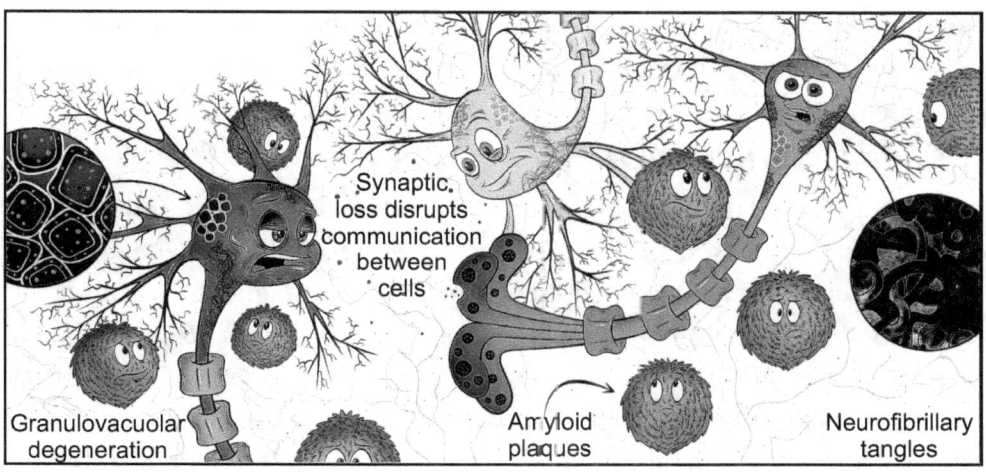

Fig. 8.2: Abnormal Structure in Alzheimer's disease

MANAGEMENT

There is no cure for Alzheimer's disease; available treatments offer moderately small symptomatic assistance but stay palliative in nature. Present treatments can be divided into pharmaceutical, psychosocial and caregiving.

MEDICATIONS

The donepezil, an acetylcholinesterase inhibitor implemented for the treatment of AD symptoms. Molecular structure of memantine, a medication permitted for higher AD symptoms. In total five medications are now used to treat the cognitive problems of AD. Out of these four are acetylcholinesterase inhibitors (tacrine, rivastigmine, galantamine and donepezil) and the (memantine) is an NMDA receptor antagonist. The advantage starting their use is little. Till date no medication has been clearly shown to delay or halt the progression of the disease.

A decline in the action of the cholinergic neurons is a well-known characteristic of Alzheimer's disease. The Acetylcholin-esterase inhibitors are engaged to diminish the rate at which acetylcholine (ACh) is destroyed at synovial joints, thereby increasing the deliberation of ACh in the brain and combating the loss of ACh due to the death of cholinergic neurons. There is confirmation for the effectiveness of these medications in mild to moderate form of AD, and some affirmation for their utilization in the advanced stage. Simply donepezil is approved for dealing of advanced AD dementia. The use of these drugs in gentle cognitive impairment has not revealed any effect in a delay of the onset of AD. The most common side effects are nausea and vomiting, both of which are allied to cholinergic overload. These side effects arise in about 10–20% of users, are mild to moderate in severity, and can be adjusted by slowly managing medication doses. Less common secondary effects include muscle cramps, decreased heart rate (bradycardia), decreased appetite and weight, and elevated gastric acid production.

PSYCHOSOCIAL INTERVENTION

A purposely designed room for sensory amalgamation therapy also called *snoezelen* an emotion oriented psychosocial intrusion for people with dementia. Psychosocial interventions are used as an attachment to pharmaceutical treatment and can be classified in behavior, emotion, cognition or stimulation oriented approaches. Research on efficiency is engaged and rarely definite to AD, focusing instead on dementia in general. The interventions are focused to recognize and decrease antecedents and penalty of behavior. Such approach has not shown achievement in civilizing overall functioning, but can assist to reduce some detailed difficulty in behaviors, such as incontinence. There is a lack of high quality data on the effectiveness of these techniques in other behavior problems such as wandering.

Emotion oriented interference embrace reminiscence (looking back, recollecting) therapy, validation therapy, supportive psychotherapy, sensory integration, also called *snoezelen*, and imitation incidence therapy. Supportive psychotherapy has established little or no official scientific study, but some clinician's find it helpful in serving mildly impaired people amend to their sickness. Reminiscence Therapy (RT) involves the discussion of past experience alone or in group, many times with the aid of photographs, household items, music and sound recordings, or other familiar items from the earlier period. Although there are few quality investigations on the usefulness of RT, it may be useful for cognition and mood. Simulated Presence Therapies (SPT) is support on attachment theories and involves playing a recording with voices of the closest relatives of the person with Alzheimer's disease. There is partial evidence indicating that SPT may reduce challenging behaviors. Lastly, validation therapy is based on recognition of the actuality and personal truth of another's skill, while sensory integration is based on workout aimed to arouse senses. There is no evidence to support the usefulness of these therapies.

CARE-GIVING

In view of the fact that Alzheimer's has no treatment and it progressively renders people unable of nurture for their own needs, care-giving fundamentally is the treatment and must be cautiously managed over the course of the illness. During the early and moderate stages, modifications to the living environment and lifestyle can boost patient safety and reduce caretaker load. Examples of such modifications are the observance to simplified routines, the placing of safety locks, the labeling of domestic items to signal the person with the disease or the use of customized daily life objects. If eating become challenging, food will need to be set in smaller pieces or even pureed. When swallowing difficulty occur, the use of feeding tubes may be obligatory. In such cases, the medical effectiveness and ethics of enduring feeding is an important contemplation of the caregivers as well as family members. The use of physical restraints is hardly ever indicated in any phase of the disease, even though there are situations when they are essential to prevent harm to the person with AD or their caregivers.

As the disease progresses, diverse medical issues can emerge, such as oral and dental disease, pressure ulcers, malnutrition, hygiene problems, or respiratory, skin or eye infections. Vigilant supervision can avoid them, while qualified treatment is desired when they do take place. During the final stages of the disease, treatment is centered on relieving distress until death.

IMPORTANCE OF LIFESTYLE

Physical and Mental Activity

Physical and mental behavior peak the record for Alzheimer's anticipation. A 2005 Finnish study showed that middle aged people who occupied in leisure-time physical activity not less than twice a week halved their likelihood of mounting the disease 20 years later. People 65 years and older who engage in 15-minute sessions of physical activity for three or more times per week condensed their possibility of dementia by about 40%. These were not seniors successively marathons: Their actions incorporated such low-impact pursuits as walking, stretching, calisthenics and swimming.

Healthy Nutrition

The role of nutrition for brain health is ongoing but, so far, has been less convincing, partly since dietary studies are disgracefully difficult to conduct. Only some people are keen to spend years on controlled diets in order to test their latent health profit. The nutritional supplement such as vitamin pills even, as easier to test, do not influence the body in the identical traditions as complete foods.

Medical Risk Factors

Lifestyle choices are the first line of defense for reducing our risk of Alzheimer's. As with other chronic diseases that excessively concern the aged, nonetheless, medical conditions can also manipulate our liability.

Be Concerned About Memory Loss?

Many people worry that Alzheimer's disease is just around the turn when they misplace their key or cannot keep in mind someone's surname. But we lose things at any age, and the "tip-of-the-tongue syndrome". Since as on date Alzheimer's is second only to cancer as the disease to fear the most.

DO'S AND DON'TS IN ALZHEIMER'S DISEASES

Do's

- Keep communication simple and questions to a least to avoid irritation.
- If they ask you the identical problem over and over, does not points out they just asked it. Keep your answer short and to the point.
- Concentrate on the skills they encompass, not the skills they have lost.
- Keep distractions at a bare minimum. Lower the volume of the television or else radio.
- Ask the caregiver what actions the patient still enjoys.
   o   Be patient.
   o   Be reassuring.

Don'ts

- Do not quiz a person with Alzheimer's as it may upset individual.
- Make eye contact, smile and hold hands. Non-verbal call is often supportive in encouraging people.
- Do not inquire them: "Do you remember who I am?" Instead of that, initiate yourself tell your link to him. For example, articulate, "Hi, Surendra Modi, It's your next door neighbor to Raul gandhi."

Chapter 9

INFERTILITY

"Sometimes its hard to see the rainbow when there's been endless days of rain".

— Christina Greer

INTRODUCTION

Infertility is the lack of ability of a person, animal or plant to reproduce by natural means. It is usually not the natural state of a healthy adult organism, except particularly among certain eusocial species (mostly haplodiploid insects). In humans, infertility may express a woman who is not capable to conceive as well as being unable to carry a pregnancy to full term. There are a lot of biological and other reasons of infertility, including few that medical intervention can indulgence. Infertility rates have been increased by 4% ever since the 1980s, mostly from problems with fecudity due to a raise in age. Around 40% of the issues concerned with infertility are owing to the man, another 40% because of the woman, and 20% result from complications with both partners. (Fig. 9.1).

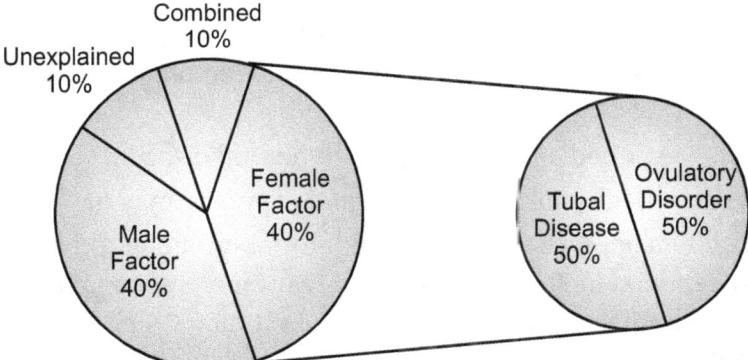

Fig. 9.1: Causes of infertility

Women who are fertile experience a natural stage of fertility prior to and throughout ovulation; moreover they are naturally infertile for the period of the rest of the menstrual cycle. Fertility awareness methods are used to discern when these changes ensue by track change in cervical mucous or basal body temperature.

The World Health Organization defines infertility as:

"The failure to achieve a clinical pregnancy after 12 months or more of regular unprotected sexual intercourse (and there is no other reason, such as breast feeding or postpartum amenorrhoea).

The most important infertility is sterility in a couple who have never had a child. Secondary infertility is failure to conceive subsequent a previous pregnancy. Infertility may be caused by contamination in the man or woman, but frequently there is no obvious fundamental origin.

Prevalence

It is a global health issue, affecting approximately 8-10% couples worldwide. The World Health Organization (WHO) estimate that 60 to 80 million couples universally at present suffer from infertility. The WHO estimates of primary infertility in India are 3.9% (age-standardized to 25-49 years) as well 16.8% (age-standardized to 15-49 years), into "age but no birth".

At the end of 2012, as stated by WHO reported, one in every four couples in developing countries had been establish to be affected by infertility. The scale of the problem calls for imperative action, mainly when in the majority of cases the infertility is preventable. Estimates of infertility vary widely among Indian states from 3.7% in Uttar Pradesh, Himachal Pradesh and Maharashtra, to 5% in Andhra Pradesh and 15% in Kashmir.

SIGNS AND SYMPTOMS OF INFERTILITY

Infertility Symptoms in Women

- Irregular periods: Hemorrhage is heavier or lighter than normal.
- Unbalanced periods: The number of days in among each period varies each month.
- No periods: Never had a period, or periods abruptly stop.
- Painful periods: Back pain, pelvic pain, and cramping may happen.
- Sometimes, female infertility is related to a hormone problem. In this case, symptoms can also include: Skin change, with more acne, alterations in sex drive and desire, dark hair growth on the lips, chest, and chin, loss of hair or thinning hair, weight put on.
- Other symptoms consist of: cloudy white discharge from nipples not linked to breast feeding, pain during sex.
- Many other things can lead to infertility in women, and their symptoms vary.

Infertility Symptoms in Men

- Alterations in hair growth.
- Escalation of sexual desire.
- Pain, lump, or swelling in the testicles.
- Problems with erections and ejaculation.
- Small, firm testicles.

MYTHS AND MISUNDERSTANDINGS OF INFERTILITY

- **Myth:** *Infertility is a women's trouble:*
- **Fact:** This is false. It is essential that both the man and the woman be evaluated during an infertility work-up.
- **Myth:** *It is all in your head! Why do not unwind or take a vacation. After that you will get expectant:*
- **Fact:** Infertility is a disease or circumstance of the reproductive system. While calming may help with overall quality of life, the strain and deep emotions we feel are the result of infertility, not the cause of it. Improved medical techniques have made it easier to identify infertility troubles.
- **Myth:** *Do not worry so much it just takes point in time. You will get pregnant if you are just patient:*
- **Fact:** Infertility is a medical problem that may be treated. In any case half of those who complete an infertility assessment will respond to deal with a successful pregnancy. Some infertility problems respond with higher or lower success rates.
- **Myth:** *If you adopt a baby you will get pregnant!*
- **Fact:** This is one of the most throbbing myths for couples to listen first it suggests that adoption is only a way to an end, not a happy and victorious end in itself. Second, it is just not true.
- **Myth:** *Why do not you just overlook it and adopt? Finally, several offspring out there who necessitate homes!*
- **Fact:** For a lot of, adoption is a happy declaration to infertility, yet, the majority people explore medical conduct for infertility former to considering adoption.
- **Myth:** *Possibly you two are doing incredible wrong!*
- **Fact:** Infertility is a medical situation, not a sexual disorder.
- **Myth:** *Partner may leave me due to our infertility.*
- **Fact:** The majority of couples do live the infertility crisis, learning in the course new ways of linking to each other, which deepens their relationship in years to go after.
- **Myth:** *Infertility is nature's way of controlling population.*
- **Fact:** Zero population expansion is goals pursue in a time of world overpopulation, except it still allow for couples to replace themselves with two children. Individuals or couples can certainly elect the option to be child free or to raise a single child.
- **Myth**: *I should not take a month off from infertility dealing for any cause... I just recognize next month will be the one!*

- **Fact:** It is vital occasionally to reconsider your treatment and parenting goal. Continuity in treatment is essential, but occasionally a break can provide desired rest and rejuvenation for the next steps.
- **Myth:** *I will be label a 'trouble maker' if I ask too many questions.*
- **Fact:** The physician/patient team is central. What is true for one couple may not be correct for another, either physically, financially, or psychologically. Do not be scared to ask question to doctor. A subsequent view can be helpful. If required, argue this alternative with your physician.
- **Myth**: *I have lost curiosity in my job, hobbies, and my friends. No one understands!*
- **Fact:** Infertility is a life predicament it has a ripple effect on all areas of your life. It is normal to feel a sense of failure that can affect your self-esteem and self-image.

CAUSES OF INFERTILITY

Male Infertility

- Abnormal sperm production due to various problems, such as underdeveloped testicles, genetic defects, health problems together with diabetes, previous infections such as mumps, trauma or earlier surgeries on the testicles or inguinal region. Enlarged veins in the testes can increase blood flow and heat, disturbing the number and shape of sperm.
- Troubles with the delivery of sperm caused by sexual problems, such as premature ejaculation, semen entering the bladder instead of rising through the penis all through orgasm (*retrograde ejaculation*), definite genetic diseases, such as cystic fibrosis, structural problems, such as blockage of the part of the testicle that contains sperm (epididymis), or injury to the reproductive organs. Men who have earlier undergone a vasectomy and desire a return of fertility will also need to either have the vasectomy reversed or have sperm retrieved in the course of a surgical process for use in assisted reproductive technique.
- Overexposure to certain chemicals and toxins, such as pesticides, radiation, tobacco smoke, alcohol, marijuana, and steroids (including testosterone). Additionally, recurrent exposure to heat, such as in saunas or hot tubs, can raise the testicular temperature, impairing sperm production.
- Damage associated to cancer along with its cure, including radiation or chemotherapy. Treatment for cancer can damage sperm creation or sperm abnormality as shown in Fig. 9.2. Elimination of one testicle due to cancer as well influences male fertility.

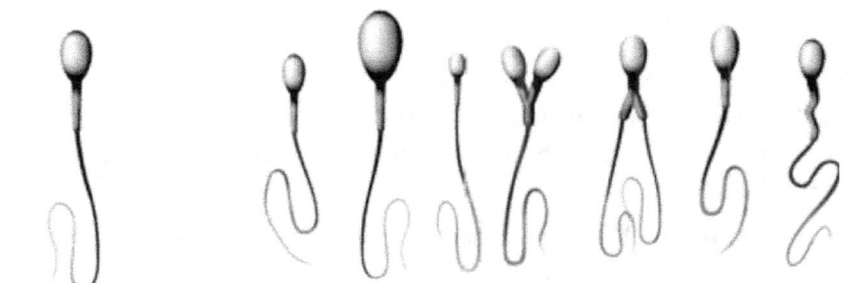

(a) **Normal Forms**   (b) **Abnormal forms**

Fig. 9.2: Sperm Structure

Female Infertility

- Ovulation disorders, which prevent the ovaries from release of eggs. For instance, hormonal disorders such as polycystic ovary condition, a situation that might relate to ovaries producing excessively much of the male hormone testosterone, in addition to hyperprolactinemia, when having excess prolactin, the hormone that stimulates production of milk in the breast. Other underlying causes may include excessive exercise, eating disorders, or tumors.

- Uterine or cervical abnormality, includes problems with the opening of the cervix or cervical mucous, or abnormality in shape or cavity of the uterus. Benign tumors in wall of the uterus are common in women (uterine fibroids) could hardly ever cause infertility by blocking the fallopian tubes. More often, fibroids may distort the uterine cavity intrusive with implantation of the fertilized egg.

- Fallopian tube blockage, which normally results from inflammation of the fallopian tube *(salpingitis)*. These can consequence start with pelvic inflammatory disease, regularly due to sexually transmitted infection, endometriosis or adhesions.

- Endometriosis occurs when endometrial tissue implants and grows exterior of the uterus, regularly disturbing the role of the ovaries, uterus and fallopian tubes.

- Primary ovarian insufficiency, also called early menopause, when the ovaries stop working and menstruation ends prior to age 40. Even though the cause is over and over again unknown, certain conditions are associated with early menopause, including immune disorder, radiation or chemotherapy therapy, and smoking.

- Pelvic adhesions, bands of scar tissue to bind organs subsequent to pelvic infection, appendicitis, or abdominal or pelvic surgery.

OTHER CAUSES IN WOMEN

Other causes in women includes:

- **Thyroid Troubles:** The disturbed thyroid gland, either hyperthyroidism (too much thyroid hormone) or hypothyroidism (too little) can disrupt the menstrual cycle or else cause infertility.
- **Cancer Treatment:** Certain cancers mainly female reproductive cancers often severely spoil female fertility. Both radiation and chemotherapy may influence a woman's capability to reproduce.
- **Other Conditions:** Medical circumstances related with delayed puberty or the lack of menstruation (amenorrhea), such as celiac disease, Cushing's disease, sickle cell disease, kidney disease, diabetes, can have an effect on a woman's fertility. In addition genetic abnormalities can make conception and pregnancy less likely.
- **Certain Medications:** The use of certain medications may cause temporary infertility. In nearly all cases, fertility is restored when the medication is stopped.

MANAGEMENT OF INFERTILITY

Lifestyle

It is necessary that patients should be optimistic to stop smoking cigarettes and marijuana and to restrict environmental exposures to harmful substances or conditions. Stress-relief therapy and consultation of proper psychological along with social professional may be advocated. Infections should be treated with right antimicrobial therapy.

IMPORTANCE OF LIFESTYLE IN INFERTILITY

Alcohol

Having two glass of wine would not have a huge impact on our fertility, but we should limit the amount of alcohol that we consume. Heavy drinking has been associated to an augmented risk of ovulation disorders along with poor sperm quality.

Smoking

Most of the people are already aware that smoking is harmful to overall health but many do not realize that it also affects fertility of a person. Smoking has major adverse effects on equally egg and sperm feature. It also decreases sperm count, rate of pregnancy along with increase in sperm DNA fragmentation, which can lead to miscarriage.

Weight

Being whichever overweight or underweight can lower the fertility rate in both men and women. Men with a high BMI be inclined to have an inferior sperm count and abridged sperm quality. Women with a high BMI are at greater risk of miscarriage, stillbirth moreover caesarean delivery.

Diet

The food that we eat or do not eat can also play an important role in fertility. For instance, women trying to conceive should not have a high protein diet; the excessive protein has been associated with decreased fertility. It has also been found that 25% of women in their child bearing years have a vitamin D deficiency that has also been coupled to lower fertility.

Caffeine

Though the proof is not absolutely believable, some research suggests that too much caffeine can reduce fertility, particularly in women. A cup of coffee or two a day would not do a great deal of harm, but it is desirable to avoid unwarranted caffeine consumption.

Exercise

Staying fit all the way through usual exercse is an important feature of a healthy lifestyle. However, when it comes to fertility it can be too much of a good thing. Extremely dynamic and everyday physical activity can lead to a lower sperm count and decreased ovulation.

DO'S AND DON'TS IN INFERTILITY

Do's

- Have regular sex, the best chance of conception comes from having unprotected intercourse twice to thrice per week. As sperm can survive inside a woman's body for two to five days. Regular intercourses increases the opportunity of sperm being there and ready to fertilize with an egg when it is free. Understand the menstrual cycle; knowing at what time our partner ovulates can help to identify right time for intercourse to increase chances of conception. Women's are most expected to conceive when she has intercourse one to two days prior to ovulation.

- Maintaining a healthy BMI, weights affect equally i.e. woman's ability to ovulate and health of a male's sperm. If partner is overweight, consider a healthy eating and exercise management.

- Start taking a folate complement. Research suggests it reduces the risk of neural tube defects, for instance spina bifida.

  Spina Bifidac Occulta (SBO) is a group of situation distressing the spinal column. The spinal column is made of bones, called "vertebrae." They support the body and protect a large group of nerves, called the "spinal cord." The spinal cord carries nerve signals from the body to the brain.

  SBO is common; 10 to 20 per cent of healthy people have it. Normally it is safe and people often tend out they have it through an X-ray. Spina Bifida Occulta usually does not cause nervous system problems (Fig. 9.3).

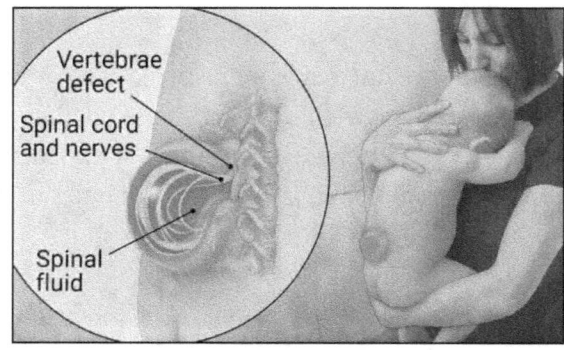

Fig. 9.3: Spina Bifidac Occulta

- Ask your doctor if you should stop taking any prescription drugs, since some can influence the health of eggs or sperm.
- Eat well. A healthy balanced diet like the Mediterranean diet will offer body with the crucial vitamins and minerals it desires to cheer ovulation or healthy sperm production.
- Be certain about adequate level of vitamin D. This vitamin is well identified for its function in bone mineral density and healthy tooth growth. As recent studies reveal that undersupplied levels can also affect fertility and conception. Studies have confirmed women undergoing IVF treatment with higher vitamin D levels are more expected to attain pregnancy.

Don'ts

- Do not smoke or take recreational drugs. Both of them can hamper the health of sperm and eggs and affect sex drive.
- Do not drink more than eight average alcoholic drinks every week.

Chapter 10

PILES

"Exercise is your King and nutrition is your Queen. Together they create your fitness Kingdom".

— *Jac Lalanne*

INTRODUCTION

Piles or Hemorrhoids are vascular structures in the anal canal. Piles can be of diverse sizes and may be internal (inside the anus) or external ones (outside the anus). Typically, internal piles arise starting above 2 to 4 cm of opening of the anus or anal canal. Whereas, the external piles (perianal hematoma) arise on the outside boundary of the anus. The internal ones are much more widespread. In their normal status, they are cushions that assist with stool control. They turn out to be pathological or piles when swollen or inflamed. At this time, the state is technically identified as hemorrhoidal disease. The signs and symptoms of depend on the type present. Internal Piles usually present with painless rectal bleeding, while external Piles may produce few symptoms or if thrombosed significant pain along with swelling in the area of the anus. Most of the inhabitants wrongly refer to any symptom occurring around the anal-rectal area as "Piles " and serious causes of the symptoms should be ruled out. While the exact cause of Piles remains unknown, a number of factors which increase intra-abdominal pressure, in particular constipation is believed to play a role in their development.

CLASSIFICATION AND GRADING OF HAEMORRHOIDS

Haemorrhoids are classified according to their origin; the dentate lines (pectinate line) serve as an anatomic-histologic border. The external haemorrhoids initiate distal to the dentate line and internal haemorrhoids originate proximal to the dentate line. In some cases the two types coexist. (As shown in Fig. 10.1).

- **External Haemorrhoids:** It begins from distal to the dentate line, arising from the inferior hemorrhoidal plexus. They are sometimes painful as lined by means of customized squamous epithelium, which is richly innervated with somatic pain fibres (delta type, unmyelinated), and often accompanied by swelling and irritation. External haemorrhoids are prone to thrombosis, they turn into thrombosed when the vein ruptures and/or a blood clot develop.

- **Internal Haemorrhoids:** Internal haemorrhoids are symptomatic, derive proximal to the dentate line, arise on or after the superior hemorrhoidal plexus, as well as are covered with mucosa. According to Golligher's classification, internal haemorrhoids are subdivided into four grades according to the extent of prolapse.

  1. **First-degree haemorrhoids:** The hemorrhoidal tissue bulges into the lumen of the anal canal, (can be inspected only, not felt) and may or may not make painless bleeding.

  2. **Second-degree haemorrhoids:** They stick out at the time of bowel movement and reduce spontaneously.

  3. **Third-degree haemorrhoids:** They are those that protrude spontaneously or at the time of bowel movement and require physical decline.

  4. **Fourth-degree haemorrhoids:** They are those that are permanently prolapsed and irreducible despite attempts at manual reduction. On source of lithotomy location, there are typically three major haemorrhoidal cushions originated to the right posterior, right anterior and left lateral position known as 3, 7 and 11 O'clock position of the anal canal.

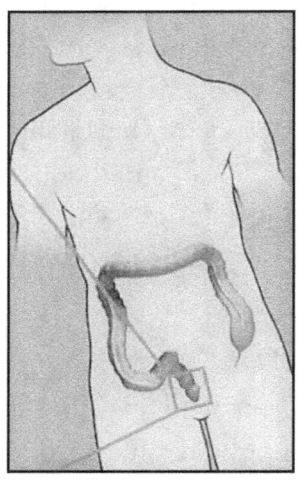

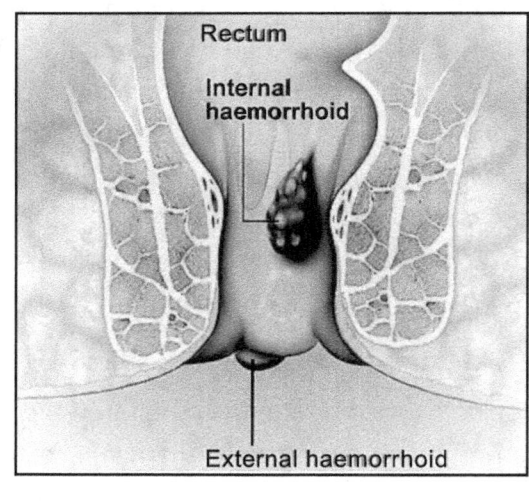

(a)   (b)

Fig. 10.1: Internal and external piles

In the early hours treatment for mild to modest disease covers increasing fibre intake, oral fluids to uphold hydration, NSAIDs to help with pain, and rest. Various trivial measures can be perform if symptoms are rigorous or do not advance with conventional management. Surgery is set aside for those who fail to improve following these measures. Up to half of people may experience problems with Piles at some point in their lives.

EPIDEMIOLOGY

It is difficult to decide how common Piles are as many people with the condition do not see a healthcare provider. Many individuals experience this condition without seeking medical consultation; patients are habitually unwilling to seek medical help due to embarrassment or the fear, uneasiness, and pain associated with the treatment, so the exact incidence of this disease cannot be estimated.

Age incidence: The age sharing of haemorrhoids verified a hyperbolic model with a peak between age of 45-65 years and a subsequent decline after the age of 65 years. In the age group of 45-65 years, it has expected that 50-85% people of world roughly have the haemorrhoids. The presence of haemorrhoids in patients less than 20 years is unusual.

Sex incidence: Approximately, the same incidences of haemorrhoids are experienced by either sexes, but if both symptomatic and asymptomatic haemorrhoids are taken into thought the presence of haemorrhoids are slightly more in males. Haemorrhoids are particularly rare in communities, which have departed least from their traditional manner of life, but more in economically developed communities. There is a close link with western type of diet, which is more refined and low in fibre rising bowel transit time and forming hard stools. There are sizeable facts that haemorrhoids become commoner with progressive adoption of a more western way of life.

Occupation People: It cover the occupation require prolong sitting (e.g. drivers, clerks etc.), standing (e.g. security guards etc.) or lifting of heavy weight (e.g. weight lifters, coolies, etc.) are at elevated threat for developing haemorrhoids. Few studies also noted that occupation stress or strain played an significant role in precipitating prolapse of existing internal haemorrhoids.

General incidence and prevalence of haemorrhoids: According to NIH data, nearly 1 million cases are reported per annum in US at the occurrence rate of 4.4%. It is estimated that 58% of people aged over 40 years have the disease in the US. Some researchers suggest that about 75% of people will have symptomatic haemorrhoids at some point of time in their lives.

In India, roughly 40,723,288 people are report to have haemorrhoids. One million new cases are reported annually, at the rate of 47 per 1000 and this rate increase through age. Recent statistics suggest nearly half of the world's population will experience some form of haemorrhoids particularly when they reach the golden age of fifty. According to several studies carried out in high-risk groups, the prevalence rate of haemorrhoids is very high.

It was felt that if the frequency of haemorrhoids in the symptomatic plus asymptomatic groups is similar or close to similar in every age. It is likely that a few people will have haemorrhoids in every age irrespective of the presence or absence of symptom.

SIGNS AND SYMPTOMS

Internal and external Piles may present differently; however, many people may have a blend of the two. Bleeding noteworthy enough to cause anemia is rare, and life-threatening bleeding is even more uncommon. Many people feel embarrassed when facing the problem and frequently seek medical care only when the case is advanced.

External: If not thrombosed, external Piles may cause few problems, however, when thrombosed piles are very painful. Nevertheless, this pain typically resolves in 2–3 days. The swelling may, however, take a few weeks to disappear. A skin tag may remain after healing. If Piles are large and cause issues with hygiene, they may make irritation of the nearby skin, and thus itchiness around the anus.

Internal: Internal Piles usually present with painless, bright red rectal bleeding during or following bowel. The blood classically covers the stool (hematochezia), is on the toilet paper, or drips into the toilet bowl. The stool itself is usually normally coloured. Other symptoms may include mucous discharge, a perianal mass if they prolapse through the anus, itchiness, and fecal incontinence. Internal Piles are usually only painful if they become thrombosed or necrotic.

CAUSES

The veins surrounding anus tend to stretch under pressure and may bulge or swell. Swollen veins (hemorrhoids) can build up from a raised pressure in lower rectum. Factors which may cause increased pressure comprises:

- Straining throughout bowel movements
- Sitting for stretched periods of time on the toilet
- Persistent diarrhoea or constipation
- Obesity
- Pregnancy
- Anal intercourse
- Low-fibre diet.

Hemorrhoids are more possible as we get older because of the tissues which hold up the veins in rectum and anus can weaken and stretch with aging.

The actual cause of hemorrhoids is not known. Few of the earliest proposed cause include temperament, body habits, customs, passions, sedentary life, tight-laced clothes, climate, as well as seasons. Hemorrhoids are regular in patients with spinal-cord injuries, chronic diarrhoea, constipation; poor bathroom habits, postponing bowel activities, and poor-fibre diet are also considered to be causative reason.

The latest investigations link with gravity intrinsic weakness of the blood vessel wall, heredity, genetic predisposition, to that of increased intra-abdominal pressure from many causes. Including prolonged forceful valsalva defecation, obstruction of venous outflow secondary on the way to pregnancy, moreover constipated stool in the rectal ampulla. Alcoholic cirrhosis or other causes of portal obstruction can lead to severe hemorrhoids. Very hardly but much notably, hemorrhoids may reflect collateral anastomotic channels that develop as a result of portal hypertension.

MANAGEMENT

Medical management is the initial treatment of choice for grade-I internal as well as non-thrombosed external hemorrhoids. It includes warm baths (two to three times daily); a high-fibre diet; adequate fluid intake; stool softeners; topical and systemic analgesics; appropriate anal sanitation; and in some cases, a short course of topical steroid cream.

Retraining the patient's toilet habit is healthy contemplation; declining straining and constipation shrink internal hemorrhoids and decrease their symptom. Consequently, first-line treatment of all first and second degree (sometimes lots of third- and fourth-degree) internal hemorrhoids is supposed to comprise events to reduce straining and constipation.

Most of the patients witness enhancement or complete resolution of symptoms with conservative measures. Aggressive therapy is reserved for patients who have determined symptoms subsequent to 1 month of conservative therapy. Treatment is heading for solely at symptoms and not at the emergence of the hemorrhoics.

Warm Baths

Bathing in tubs with warm water commonly eases painful perianal circumstances. Relaxation of sphincter means and spasm is most likely the etiology. Ice can alleviate the pain of acute thrombosis. Few authors do not propose mechanisms like the sitz bath for indication relief. The inflexible structure of these portable bathing apparatus can act in a similar style as a toilet seat, cause venous congestion in the perianal area and potentially exacerbating the crisis. However, sitz baths do have a role in the treatment of older or immobile patients who cannot usually capable of using bath tub.

High Fibre Diet

Psyllium seed drastically reduces bleeding and pain compare to placebo. Psyllium seed (Metamucil) and methylcellulose (Citrucel) are the most normally used supplements. The normal American diet consists of 8-15 g of fibre/day; a high fibre diet include above 25 g of fibre/day. Many hemorrhoidal symptoms resolve only when they are treated with dietary alteration, together with augmented fibre and the addition of fibre supplement.

Antidiarrhoeal Agents, Toilet Habit Retraining, or Stool Softeners

Antidiarrheal agents are rarely necessary in patients with hemorrhoidal symptoms and loose stools. Toilet retraining involves reminding that the lavatory is not the library. Patients must sit on the toilet simply long enough to empty the lower intestines. Constant straining or prolonged sitting can lead to engorged hemorrhoids.

Stool softeners play a limited role in the treatment of regular hemorrhoidal symptoms. Oral fibre eating along with fibre supplements approximately for all time cure constipation and straining. Keep in mind that hemorrhoidal symptoms are due to prolapse, thrombosis, and vascular bleeding. Hence, creams or salves has little role in hemorrhoidal grievance, suppositories, except for providing lubrication; also have a small part in the treatment of hemorrhoidal symptoms.

Topical Agents

The effect of topical steroids has not been very well investigated in the treatment of thrombosed hemorrhoids; however, these agents can be use to reduce symptom of pruritus and inflammation. Topical hydrocortisone can now and then ease internal hemorrhoidal bleeding. It is vital to believe the principles of steroid use and the allied side effects, for instance mucosal atrophy.

As such, the extended use of topical steroids ought to be avoided. Rarely recommend typical medications (e.g, suppository, cream, enema, foam) in the conduct of hemorrhoids. Submucosal veins do not get smaller with anti-inflammatory medication. Topical nitroglycerine and nifedipine has also used to allay symptoms related with anal sphincter spasm. These agents should also be used with care due to related side effects, like hypotension. Good confirmation suggests that high-fibre diets in particular help ease severity and duration of symptoms.

Importance of Lifestyle

Since, shearing action of passing hard stool on the anal mucosa may cause damage to anal cushions as well as lead to symptomatic hemorrhoids, mounting intake of fibre or providing added bulk in the diet might help get rid of straining during defecation. In scientific studies of hemorrhoids, fibre supplement condensed the hazard of persisting symptoms and bleeding by approximately 50%, but did not improve the symptoms of prolapse, pain, and itching. Fibre supplement is so regard as an effective treatment in non-prolapsing hemorrhoids; yet, it could take up to 6 weeks for a significant progress to be evident. As fibre supplements are safe and cheap, they remain an integral part of both initial treatment and schedule subsequent additional beneficial modalities of hemorrhoids.

Lifestyle alteration should also be suggested to any patients with any degree of hemorrhoids as a part of treatment and as a preventive measure. Such changes comprise increasing the intake of dietary fibre and oral fluids, reducing consumption of fat, having usual exercise, improving anal hygiene, abstaining from both straining and reading on the toilet, and avoiding medication that causes constipation or diarrhoea.

DO'S AND DON'TS IN PILES

Do's

- Use high roughage diet with high-fibre content.
- Drink lots of fluids to avoid constipation.
- Lose weight, if overweight.
- Exercise on a regular basis.
- In pregnancy, exercise should be in proper supervision and guidance.
- Itchiness and pain can be calmed by having hot baths.
- Employ moist wipes, as a substitute of rough toilet paper.
- Take proper medications to control chronic cough.

Don'ts

- Avoid prolonged sitting on the toilet seat.
- Do not strain at stool.
- Do not pull at urination.
- Avoid prolonged sitting at work. Get up and move around periodically.
- Avoid lifting or holding heavy objects.
- Avoid overuse of laxatives or enemas.

Chapter 11

ADDICTION

"Addiction begins with the hope that something 'out there' can instantly fill up the emptiness inside."

— *Jean Kilbourne*

INTRODUCTION

Addiction is a condition characterized by obsessive engagement in pleasing stimuli, regardless of adverse consequences. It can be thought of as a disease or biological process leading to such behaviors. The two features that describe all addictive stimuli are like they are *reinforcing* (i.e., they increase the likelihood that a person will seek repeated exposure to them) and intrinsically *rewarding* (i.e., a little perceived as being positive or desirable).

Addiction extracts a high toll on individuals and society as a whole through the direct adverse effects of drugs, related healthcare costs, long-term complication (e.g., lung cancer with smoking tobacco, liver cirrhosis with drinking alcohol, or meth mouth from intravenous methamphetamine), the functional penalty of altered neural plasticity in the brain, and the consequent hammering or loss of productivity. Classic hallmarks of addiction include impaired control over substances or behavior, anxiety with substance or behavior, along with continued use in despite consequences. Habits and patterns associated with addiction are typically characterized by immediate gratification (short-term reward), coupled with delayed harmful effects (long-term costs).

The examples of drug and behavioral addictions includes: alcoholism, amphetamine or cocaine opiate, nicotine, exercise, food, gambling, and sexual addictions. The only behavioral addiction recognized by the DSM-5 is gambling addiction. The term addiction is misused regularly to submit to other compulsive behaviors or disorders, mainly dependence, in news media.

LIST OF ADDICTIONS TO SUBSTANCES

- Alcohol
- Tobacco
- Opioids (like heroin)
- Prescription drugs (sedatives, hypnotics, or anxiolytics)
- Cocaine

- Cannabis (marijuana)
- Amphetamines
- Hallucinogens
- Inhalants
- Phencyclidine (known as Angeldust)
- Other unspecified substances.

ALCOHOL ADDICTION

Alcoholism is a serious medical disease with signs and symptoms that differ depending on quantity and promptness of use. Succeeding alcoholism will noticeably disrupt the life of users and their family. Physical symbols of alcohol over consumption and intoxication are recognizable by the majority of adults:

- Slurred or jumbled speech
- Poor balance and clumsiness
- Delayed reflexes
- Stomach pains, vomiting or nausea
- Loss of awareness or blacking-out
- Redness of the face throughout or after periods of use
- It is possible for a person to reach a level of intoxication that becomes life-threatening (alcohol poisoning). The respiratory organ become depressed and the person may stop breathing.

SIGNS OF ALCOHOL ABUSE

An escalating increase in the incidence and quantity of alcohol use can begin to produce more serious medical symptoms of alcoholism. The person abusing alcohol keeps drinking a central activity of life, displacing healthy activity and relationships, and ensuing in negative consequences. The alcohol abusers often retain some ability to recognize situations that lead to over-consumption, and to regulate their alcohol intake. The various signs of alcohol abuse includes:

- Loss of power over amount consumption once they begin drinking.
- Regular negligence to family along with professional obligations.
- Dangerous behaviors that carry risk of legal, financial, social or health consequences for abuser and others.
- An enhanced in expressions of anger or additional emotions, particularly in unsuitable settings.
- Insomnia, that followed by oversleep.

Signs of Dependence (i.e. Alcoholism)

Untreated alcohol abuse can steps forward to an addiction to alcohol characterize by physical addiction and/or inability to stop regardless of serious consequences. Once they begin drinking, alcoholics have modest to no power over quantity of sip. Alcohol dependence indicates that the user has made obtaining and consuming alcohol a predominant focus of life.

Signs and symptoms of alcohol dependence symbolize a serious medical illness:

- Significant hangovers, and increase in time needed to recover from after effects of alcohol use.
- Increased quantity of alcohol consumption due to increased tolerance; or, decrease in the effects of alcohol use without extensive increases in the amount consumed.
- Reduced attention to personal and professional duties.
- Acknowledgement of side effects of medical complications from alcoholism.
- Repeated abortive efforts to reduce alcohol consumption.
- Withdrawal symptoms while incapable to drink alcohol.

Long-term alcohol abuse and addiction put at high risk for serious medical penalty if they try to stop alcohol use devoid of medical counsel and direction. Alcoholism withdrawal symptoms point to advanced addictive disease, and must not be dismissed:

- Tremors, convulsions, or uncontrolled shivering of the hands (or whole body).
- Copious sweating, in cold circumstances also.
- Tremendous agitation or anxiety.
- Constant insomnia.
- Nausea or else vomiting.
- Seizures.
- Hallucinations.

Alcohol detoxification is poses bigger health risks than other drugs. An abrupt discontinuation of alcohol use can frequently make a condition called as delirium tremens. An individual can pass away as a direct consequence of alcohol removal. Normally, medical detoxification is desirable to safely cessation of heavy drinking.

Effects of Alcohol Abuse and Alcohol Addiction

Long-term alcohol exploitation poses huge danger to an alcoholic's physical, mental, emotional, social moreover spiritual health. Besides too severe ramifications for the user's career, family and friends, alcoholism can cause irreparable harm to critical organs in addition to body systems:

- Liver
- Nervous system
- Heart
- Stomach (intestines)
- Brain.

Alcohol abuse and dependence also make extra medical side effects. Alcoholics often attribute this complication to other health conditions, as they attempt to avoid possession of the penalty of drinking. Common medical side effects includes:

- High blood pressure
- Sexual troubles
- Cancer
- Stomach problems
- Osteoporosis, especially in women.

Alcoholism frequently causes rigorous social complications on a person's life as well. Being drunk or hung over at employment repeatedly results in termination from an occupation, leaving a person and her dependents in severe financial difficulty. Domestic violence, marital conflict, legal problems and isolation from friends and family are also general fallout of alcohol abuse, which may be worsened by the presence of co-occurring anorexia or bulimia.

How Alcohol Affect Body?

The effect of alcohol is dwell in nature, at small quantity act as stimulant initially and at high doses produce central nervous system depressant. It has a multifaceted mode of action as well as affects multiple systems in the brain. Most notably alcohol works by binding to GABA receptors in the brain and activating the release of the chief inhibitory neurotransmitter in the central nervous system. This aspect of alcohol's physiological effects is one reason, alcohol detoxification can be dangerous. Alcohol is metabolized by the liver; hence long term consumption in excessive amounts lead to irreversible damage of the liver.

Alcohol addiction, or alcoholism, is medically diagnosed as a illness that manifest in the frequent use of alcohol, despite the negative consequences on person's life. It is one of the leading causes of death in teenagers due to overdrinking related motor vehicle accidents.

It is often evident that a person suffers financially from alcoholism in addition to these both mental and physical health suffers directly. The drinking patterns are not the same for every alcoholic in some people they get drunk every day, whereas others binge drink at particular times depending on their emotional state.

Lifestyle Modification of Alcoholism

In order to manage your disease you will have to make some permanent changes in your lifestyle. The following strategies can help you stay away from alcohol and reduce your risk of relapse:

- Socialize without alcohol.
- Avoid going to bars.
- Do not maintain alcohol at home.
- Stay away from situations and people which encourage drinking.
- Make new, non-drinking friends.
- Do fun things that do not involve alcohol.
- Avoid reaching for a drink when upset.
- Keep on presence with support groups.
- Identify your potential relapse triggers and develop coping strategies for difficult situations.
- If you have a reversion, do not get depressed, get help.
- Learn some of the stress reduction techniques, like deep breathing, meditation, yoga, regular exercise, rest, and relaxation.
- Eat a healthful and nutritious diet.

TOBACCO ADDICTION

Tobacco is one of the most commonly abused substances in the world. It is highly addictive. Although tobacco use appears to be on the decline in the United States, the Centers for Disease Control and Prevention (CDC) estimate that almost 20% of adults still smoke. This is despite nearly 70% of smokers wants to quit.

Nicotine, the major addictive substance in tobacco, causes a rush of adrenaline when absorbed in blood stream or inhaled via cigarette smoke. Nicotine also triggers a boost in dopamine the brain's "happy" chemical. This stimulates the region of the brain related to pleasure and reward. As that of any other drug, use of tobacco over time can lead to physical as well as psychological addiction. This is furthermore true for smokeless forms of tobacco, for example, snuff and chewing tobacco.

Prevalence of Tobacco and Nicotine Addiction

India has the world's second largest population, and is projected to surpass China in population by mid-century. In India, tobacco is utilized equally in smoked and smokeless forms. Indians smoke tobacco mainly in the form of beedis and cigarettes. The Indian beedi consists of shredded, sun-dried tobacco in small quantities that are hand rolled into a piece of leaf called tendu.

Beedis are popular in India and beedi smoking starts at an early age. The smokeless forms of tobacco use in India consist of chewing tobacco along with inhalation of snuff. Chewing tobacco is mainly consumed in the form of gutkha and zarda. Gutkha, a sweetened blend of tobacco, betel, and catechu, is sold in brilliantly decorated packets; regularly used by women and children, chewed and then spit out. Zarda, a dried and coloured residual tobacco, is obtain by boiling tobacco leaves by spices in addition to lime.

Cross-sectional analysis has provided information about the incidence of tobacco use in the common population of India. The National Family Health Survey provides data from 301,984 adults in 26 Indian states in 1999. In th s notable sample, the overall prevalence was 18.4% for tobacco smoking and 21% for tobacco chewing. As compared to men, Indian women were least expected to smoke tobacco (3.4% versus 33.3%), chew tobacco (13% versus 29%), or use tobacco in both forms (15.5% versus 50.2%). Per capita burning up data suggests that beedi smoking has been progressively mounting during the past quite a few decades (World Health Organization [WHO], 1997).

Causes

Nicotine is the chemical in tobacco that keeps you smoking. It is very addictive when delivered to the lungs by inhaling tobacco smoke. It increases the release of brain chemicals called neurotransmitters, which help to regulate mood and behaviour. One of the neurotransmitters is dopamine, which may advance mood and activate observation of pleasure. Experiencing these effects from nicotine in tobacco is what makes tobacco so addictive. The nicotine addictions involve behavioural along with physical factor that are link among smoking includes:

- Certain times of the day, such as first thing in the morning, with morning coffee or through breaks at work.
- Subsequent to a meal in lunch time
- Consumption alcohol
- Certain places or friends
- Talking on the phone

- Stressful situations or when you are feeling down
- A view or smell of a flame cigarette
- Driving of car for long distance

To overcome dependence of tobacco, person needs to deal with the behaviors and routines that you correlate with smoking.

Symptoms

A tobacco addiction is harder to hide than other addictions, since it is legal, easily obtained, and can be consumed at any place and handy. In addition, the smell of the addiction follows the smoker in hair and clothing. While some individuals can smoke socially or occasionally, others become addicted. An addiction may be present if the person cannot stop smoking or chewing or attempts to quit. The withdrawal symptoms when he or she tries to quit (shaky hands, sweating, irritability, or rapid heart rate).

Hence, the person must smoke or chew after every meal or after a movie or work meeting needs tobacco products to feel "normal". For such individuals during times of stress smoking or tobacco chewing become unavoidable and essential, hence in such scenario tobacco use or smoking should not be permitted even if the person suffer with some of the health problems.

Risk Factor

Anyone that smokes or uses another type of tobacco substance is at high risk for developing dependence. Factors that direct nicotine dependence comprises are as follows:

- **Genetics:** The genes you inherit play a role in some aspects of nicotine addiction. The option that will switch on smoking and disliking of smoking habit may be partly inherited. The genetic factors may influence how receptors on the surface of brain's nerve cells react to high dose of nicotine via cigarettes.
- **Home and peer pressure:** Children who grow up with parents who smoke are more likely to become smokers. Children with friends who smoke as well are more expected to try cigarettes. Facts suggest that smoking exposed in movies and on the Internet can give confidence to young people to smoke.
- **Age:** Most people begin smoking at some stage either in childhood or in teen age lifespan. The younger one commences smoking, the greater the chances that in future turn out to be a heavy smoker as an adult.
- **Depression or mental illness:** Individuals who have depression, schizophrenia, post-traumatic stress disorder or other forms of mental illness are further likely to be smokers.
- **Substance use:** People who misuse alcohol and illegal drugs are more probably become smoker.

Complications

Tobacco smoke contains more than 60 known cancer-causing chemicals along with thousands of other harmful elements. Even "all natural" or herbal cigarettes have chemicals that are harmful to our health. When we inhale tobacco smoke, (whether actively or passively) take in this chemical that reaches to most of body's vital organs. Smoking harms almost every organ of our body, and more than 60% of people who continue smoking will die due to it. Women smokers are now at identical risk to men for dying from diseases caused by tobacco.

The various negative health effects take account of are as follows:

- **Lung Cancer and Other Lung Diseases:** Smoking results almost 9 out of 10 lung cancer cases, on top of other lung diseases, such as emphysema, chronic bronchitis, smoking also makes asthma worse.

- **Other Cancers:** Smoking is a major basis of cancers of the throat (pharynx), larynx, mouth and oesophagus, and is interrelated to cancers of the bladder, pancreas, kidney and cervix, along with some leukemias.

- **Heart and Circulatory System Problems:** Smoking increase the risk of dying due to heart and blood vessel complications (i.e. cardiovascular disease), together with heart attack along with stroke. Constant smoking just one to four cigarettes on daily basis amplify risk of heart disease. The person having heart or blood vessel disease, such as heart failure, smoking worsens condition. However, stopping smoking decreases the risk of heart attack by 50% in the first year of cessation.

- **Diabetes:** Smoking elevates the insulin resistance that can set the stage for the development of type 2 diabetes. If you have diabetes, smoking can speed the advancement of difficulties, for instance kidney disease and eye trouble.

- **Eye Problems:** Smoking can augment risk of serious eye problems like cataracts and loss of eyesight from macular degeneration.

- **Infertility with Impotence:** Smoking promotes the threat of infertility in women in addition to the jeopardy of impotence in men.

- **Pregnancy and Newborn Complications:** A mother that smokes while pregnant face a greater chance of miscarriage, preterm delivery, low birth weight and sudden infant death syndrome in newborn.

- **Cold, Flu and Other Illnesses:** Smokers are more prone to respiratory infections, such as colds, flu in addition to bronchitis.

- **Weakened Senses:** Smoking deadens our senses of taste and smell, so food is not taste as delicious as that to non-smoker.

- **Teeth and Gum Disease:** Smoking is associated with an increased risk of early gingivitis (inflammation of the gum) with a serious gum infection periodontitis, which can destroy the support system for teeth.
- **Physical Appearance:** The chemicals in tobacco smoke can change the composition of our skin, leading to premature aging and wrinkles. Smoking also yellows our teeth, fingers in addition to finger nails.
- **Risks to Family:** Non-smoking spouses and partners of smokers are privileged for risk of lung cancer and heart disease compare to people who don't live with a smoker. If you smoke, your children will be more prone to aggravation of asthma, ear infections and colds.

Psychological and Behavioral Treatments

Some tobacco users encompass accomplishment with method akin to hypnotherapy, cognitive-behavioral therapy, or neuro-linguistic programming. These help the user to modify their opinion about addiction and work to alter approach or behaviors the brain acquaintances with tobacco use.

In most cases, treatment for tobacco addiction necessitates a blend of methods and will differ from one person to the next. Individuals should talk to their doctor when medication to guarantee the safety and efficacy of treatment. The doctor may also have good treatment advice.

Prevention

The best way to avoid tobacco dependence is to not smoke during the first place. The best way to put off children from smoking is to not smoke our self. If you are a parent who smokes, the younger your children are when you quit, the less to be expected to become smokers themselves. Although you don't smoke, here are some things you might attempt as a parent:

- Promote smoke free environments. Support legislation to create each and every workplace smoke free. Encourage smoke free public spaces, together with restaurants or other places where your teen may work.
- Support legislation to increase taxes on tobacco products. Higher prices dispirit teens from starting to smoke. Higher prices on tobacco commodities, coupled with smoke free workplace laws, are the largely efficient public health policies to decrease smoking in adults as well as put off young people instigation of ever starting.
- Talk to our teenagers. An enquiry whether their friends smoke gives idea about lifestyle of our wards. Since, the majority teenagers smoke their first cigarette with a friend who already smokes. Let your child know that other types of tobacco, including cigars and smokeless tobacco, also carry considerable health risks.

- Learn what your children think about smoking. Ask them to read this article so that you can talk about it. You can be a great persuade on whether children smoke, regardless of what they see in movies and on internet.
- Help children to explore personal view. Use non-judgmental questions and practise with them how they could handle dangerous situation regarding peer pressure and smoking.
- Note the social repercussions. Remind your teenager that smoking give bad breath and make hair and clothes smell.
- Work with your schools. Become active in community and school stop-smoking programs.

Prevention of tobacco use in young people appears to be the single opportunity for preventing non-communicable disease in the world today. Therefore consumption of tobacco, among school students should be considered as a matter of great concern which requires holistic understanding. Government and Non-government institutions need to develop expertise in research, planning, designing and implementing of need-based interventions, fund raising and in working with all those sectors needing activation for effective tobacco control. More and more NGOs should be involved in tobacco control program as NGOs have expertise in advocacy, judicial intervention, youth intervention, community intervention, consumer movement, in developing material for advocacy and in media advocacy. But unfortunately, in India, only a few NGOs are involved in tobacco control program. There is need to enhance the involvement of more NGOs.

Chapter 12

DEPRESSION

"There are wounds that never show on the body that are deeper and more hurtful than anything that bleeds."

— *Laurell K. Hamilton*

INTRODUCTION

Depression is a condition of low mood and dislike to activity that can influence a person's thoughts, behavior, mind-set and sense of well-being. People with unhappy mood can feel sadness, anxious, vacant, hopeless, helpless, rubbish, guilty, irritable, humiliated or agitated. They may lose curiosity in activities that were once pleasing practice, loss of hunger or overeating, have problems in focused thinking, recall details or making decisions, and may reflect, try or commit suicide. Insomnia, too much sleeping, fatigue, ache, pains, digestive troubles or compact energy may also be present. Depressed mood is a trait of some psychiatric syndromes, for example, major depressive disorder, but it may also be a regular reaction to life measures such as grief, a sign of some bodily ailment or a side effect of some drugs and medical treatment.

PREVALANCE

In newly conducted world mental health surveys, signify that major depression is experienced in 10-15% people during lifetime and about 5% suffer from major depression in any given year. The lifetime occurrence of all depressive disorders taken together is over 20% i.e. one in five individuals. In Indian context, a recent large section survey with meticulous methodology reported generally prevalence of 15.9% for depression, which is comparable to western figures. Studies completed in primary healthcare settings in India have found depression in 21-84% of the cases.

The average age of onset for major depression is 24 years as per the recent epidemiological research, though it can begin at anytime throughout the lifespan. One of the consistent findings across almost all research studies is that women are twice as likely to have depression compared to males. Depression is much more likely among people who are unmarried, widowed, divorced or separated, or without close inter-personal relationships. Those residing in nuclear families and urban areas are possibly at a higher risk. Elderly age and presence of medical disorders pose an even higher risk of depression. Major depression is one of the chiefly recurrent mental disorders in the United States. As per the World Health Organization (WHO; 2010), key depression also bear the heaviest load of disability among mental and behavioral disorder.

SIGNS AND SYMPTOMS OF DEPRESSION

- **Feelings of Helplessness and Hopelessness:** A miserable outlook, not anything will ever get better and there is nothing you can do to recover the situation.

- **Loss of Interest in Daily Activities:** No concern in past hobby, pastimes, social actions, or sex. Loosing ability to sense joy and pleasure.

- **Appetite or Weight Changes:** Significant weight loss or weight gain, a alteration of more than 5% of body weight in a month.

- **Sleep Changes:** Especially waking up during before time hours of the morning either (insomnia), or oversleeping (hypersomnia).

- **Anger or Irritability:** Feeling nervous, restless, or even violent. The patience level is low, short temper, and everything along with everyone get on your nerves.

- **Loss of Energy:** Feeling tired, lethargic, and physically shattered. Your whole body may consider heavy, and even small everyday jobs are very tiring or take longer to complete.

- **Self-loathing:** Strong feelings of worthlessness or guilt. You insensitively criticize yourself for apparent faults and mistakes.

- **Irresponsible Behavior:** You engage in escapist behavior such as substance abuse, neurotic gambling, wild driving, or dangerous games.

- **Concentration Troubles:** Trouble in focusing, making decision, or recollection of things.

- **Unexplained Aches and Pains:** An increase in physical complaints such as headaches, back pain, aching muscles, and stomach pain.

COMMON MYTHS AND MISUNDERSTANDINGS OF DEPRESSION

Depression and sadness are one and the same.

While an overwhelming sense of sadness s often a symptom of depression, it is not synonymous with it. Sadness is momentary and provisional. Sadness is catalyzed by upsetting life experience and influential memories, but it comes and goes, it is not steady. Depression, on the other hand, is a chronic condition. The deep sadness depressed people feel does not weaken on own, and sadness is far from the only negative emotion.

It is a sign of mental weakness.

This stigma is one of the key reasons why so many people elect to experience in silence before seek help. However, no one choose to build-up depression. It is a complex mental disorder that affects a person biologically, psychologically and socially, and does not discriminate.

It is at all times brought on by shocking life events.

While certain situation can (and often do) trigger depressive episodes, the events themselves cannot take all blame for a person's depression. Loss of a loved one, divorce moreover other upsetting life experiences will leave any emotionally sensitive person feeling sad, remorseful, lonely and empty. However, those who are truly depressed find their symptoms lasting longer than two weeks and reoccurring frequently.

It is not an actual illness.

While its symptoms may be difficult to identify and it does not boast a "one size fits all" action, depression is a serious medical condition. People with depression in fact have physical difference in brain, neurotransmitter and hormone imbalances that determine the condition, not to mention its severity. Depression, like many illnesses, affects a person on every level, from their moods to their thoughts to their physical existence.

It is all in your head.

Emotional symptom is a lot thought of as the main features allied with depression, but it doesn't stop there. Most of the people with depression found to be cope up with time.

Real men do not get depressed.

Just because women are twice as likely to develop depression does not mean men should suffer in silence. In fact, middle-aged men have experienced the greatest increase in number of suicides committed each year, and the majority of them can be linked back to depression. Men often express depression differently than women, which make depression among men easier for society to overlook. Afraid of appearing less manly, strong and stable, men frequently feel less able to speak up to receive help needed. This makes depression even more dangerous for men, because they avoid treatment.

If your parents have it, you will, too.

While a genetic tendency to depression can increase a individual's possibility of developing the condition but risk is relatively small (i.e. 10 to 15 %).

CAUSES OF DEPRESSION

- **Abuse:** Past physical, sexual, or emotional abuse can cause depression afterward in life.
- **Certain Medications:** Some drugs, for instance acutance (used to treat acne), the antiviral drug interferon-alpha, as well as corticosteroids, can increase risk of depression.
- **Conflict:** Depression in people that has the biological vulnerability to develop depression may result from personal conflicts/disputes with family or friends.

- **Death or a Loss:** Sadness or grief from the death or loss of a loved one, even if natural, may boost the risk of depression.

- **Genetics:** A family history of depression may amplify the risk, is a complex trait that may be inherited across generations. Although the genetics of psychiatric disorders are not as simple as in purely genetic diseases such as Huntington's or cystic fibrosis.

- **Major Events:** Even good actions like starting a new job, graduating, or getting married can lead to depression. So can be same case with, losing a job or income, getting divorced, or retiring etc.

- **Other Personal Problems:** Problems for instance social isolation owing to other mental illnesses or being cast out of a family can guide to depression.

- **Serious Illnesses:** Occasionally depression co-exists with a major illness or is a response to the illness.

- **Substance Abuse:** Nearly 30% of people with substance exploitation troubles also have major or clinical depression.

LIFESTYLE INTERVENTIONS IN DEPRESSION

Treating depression effectively means doing more than taking your medications and going to therapy. The more you adapt your lifestyle to guarantee our body and mind are healthy, more skillful you will become at responding to challenges of depression. As always, consult with doctor before making any changes.

Following are some of the ways to improve lifestyle to balance depression.

Healthy Eating

The easiest way to improve your diet is to cut out the junk. Avoiding foods high in refined sugar, and foods packed with saturated fats should be your first step. Begin incorporating healthy foods. Some of those foods include:

(a) Fatty Acids

Two of the types of fatty acid found in our diet are omega-3 and omega-6, which can be found in fish, nuts, fresh fruits and vegetables, and olive oil.

(b) Amino Acids

The messengers within the brain, called neurotransmitters, are made of amino acids. Levels of several neurotransmitters are related to mental health, so include amino acid rich foods, such as meat, dairy products, and certain fruits and vegetables in your diet.

(c) Complex Carbohydrates

Some research suggests that eating carbohydrates actually help to stimulate the production of the feel-good neurotransmitter serotonin. Carbohydrates also assist the body to absorb the amino acid tryptophan more efficiently and the brain runs on glucose, which is resultant from carbohydrates. Complex carbohydrates can be found in whole grains, legumes, vegetables such as spinach and broccoli, and fruits such as oranges and pears.

Exercise

Exercise increases body's production of natural antidepressants. A study at Duke University shows that a lot of people who exercise 30 minutes daily for four months experienced alleviate depression devoid of any medications. Exercise reduces stress, improves mood, boost self-esteem, and provide peaceful sleep.

Weight Loss

Losing weight not only improves self-esteem and overall health, but also might give our mind the boost it needs. We do not have to starve our self on a fad diet. Eating right and exercising habitually is the tried and true method for losing weight and keeping it off. The more you incorporate those two things into your lifestyle, the more likely you will be able to stick with them.

Meditation

Meditation is the practice of appealing in a mental exercise such as deep breathing or replication of a phrase (mantra), to attain some kind of advantage. The aim in the Buddhist custom, where meditation is embedded, has been spiritual enlightenment. However, modern practices also focus on stress relief and relaxation. Meditation can help relieve anxiety that from time to time accompany depression. If depression is troublesome a person's sleep habits, deep-breathing techniques can help to calm the mind in order to sleep healthier.

Sleep

A common complication of depression is lack of sleep. When we lie awake in bed at night with a brain that will not calm down or wakening in the middle of the night and cannot get back to sleep. Fatigue from a lack of sleep may add to the symptoms of depression. Proper sleep sanitation is an important part of a depression handling plan. Having a calming bed time practice that helps to wind down and subsequent a reliable sleep schedule can help to pick up the amount and quality of sleep.

Relationships

Depression can be alienating, but the true network of friends and loved ones can assist to conquer problems. Spending time with positive, supportive, and loving people can help through darkest times.

Stress Management

Stress is a component of life, but chronic, long-term stress can be devastating, particularly for someone with depression. Because stress builds upon itself, it is essential to regularly combat stress with calming, soothing experiences.

DO'S AND DON'TS IN DEPRESSION

Do's

- Recognize that depression by itself appears to be a risk factor for heart disease, one that may be modifiable, by aggressive treatment of the mood disorder.
- Get as much exercise as possible. Exercises combat both depression plus heart disease directly. It creates alteration in brain cells. It improves blood lipid levels and counters the inclination to obesity that may direct to heart disease.
- Disburse special thought to diet and curb the intake of saturated fats. It is necessary to preserve blood flow to your heart and to your brain. Plus it influence the work of nerve cell membranes.
- Increase consumption of omega-3 fats. They seem to have specific effects on many of the mechanisms of heart disease concerned in depressed people.
- Cut down on use of omega-6 fats, usually found in fried and processed foods, which rely on soy and corn oils.
- Develop a variety of ways of tackling stress even during remission. Stress can be blocked on the way by meditation, its impact blunted via exercise. It is stress overwhelms coping resources that depression results.
- Support anybody close to you who suffers a heart attack to feel a formal psychiatric assessment. Recognition and treatment of depression are the new standard of care.
- Recognize that while older antidepressants are cardiotoxic, the newer antidepressants, notably the Selective Serotonin Reuptake Inhibitors, have been prove safe for handling of depression in the presence of heart disease.

Don'ts

- Don't holdup handlings for depression, as it emerge to be a strong independent risk factor? The longer depression exists, the harder it to cure and the more deep rooted the risk.
- Don't patch up for less than hostile treatment of depressive symptoms. The goal is complete return of well-being. It may take total elimination of depressive symptoms to reduce the risk of reversion or of heart disease.
- Don't just take care of depression. Proof so far suggest that you also need to specifically battle the risk of heart disease on several fronts.

- Don't just limit intake of saturated fats. Be convinced to utilize monounsaturated fats (olive oil) and to consume liberal amounts of omega-3 type of polyunsaturated fats, found most richly in ocean fish. The American Heart Association recommends 2-3 times fish a week to avert heart disease, 1 gram a day for cardiac patients.

- Don't let the inertia and withdrawal bent by the state stop from serving someone who is depressed. The most excellent thing you can do is take them out for walks regularly, 30 minutes at least three times /week. Exercise directly and not directly counter the identified risk factors for heart disease in depressed people.

- Don't ignore signs of depression after a cardiac circumstance. It is common after a heart attack, and is the single main predictor of survival. Do look for treatment of the depression and other specific cardiac risk factors.

Chapter 13

STROKE

"Start thinking wellness, not illness"

– Kate Allatt,

INTRODUCTION

Stroke is also called as cerebrovascular accident, cerebrovascular insult, or brain attack, is while poor bloods flow to the brain fallout in cell death. There are two main types of strokes: ischemic, owing to lack of blood flow, and hemorrhagic in consequence of bleeding. They result in part of the brain not working appropriately. The stroke victim may include incapacity to move or feel on one side of the body, problems indulgent or talking, feeling like the world is rotating, or loss of vision to one side among others.

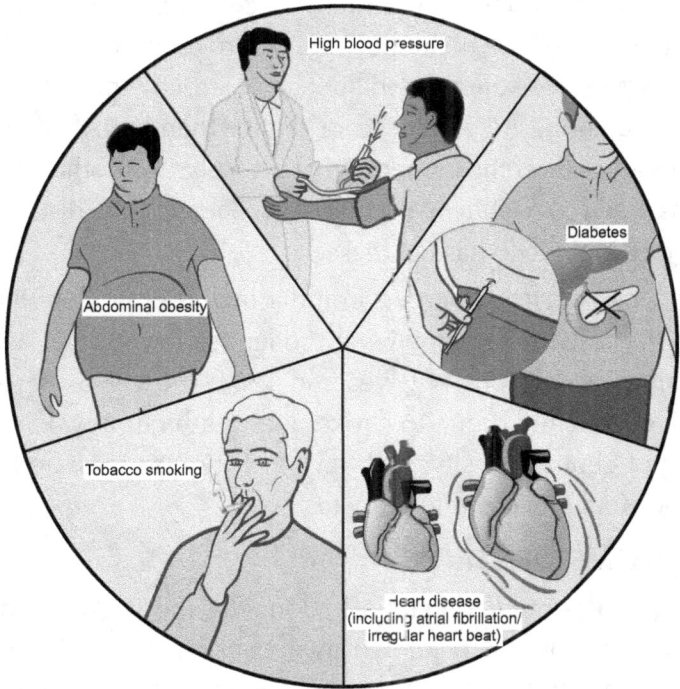

Fig. 13.1: Cardinal risk factor for stroke

The main cardinal risk factor for stroke is high blood pressure, high blood cholesterol, diabetes mellitus, tobacco smoking, obesity, previous transient ischemic attack, and atrial fibrillation between others. An ischemic stroke is typically caused by blockage of a blood vessel. A hemorrhagic stroke is caused by bleeding either directly into brain or into space surrounding the brain. Bleeding may occur due to a brain aneurysm. Identification is normally with medical imaging for instance a CT scan or MRI scans beside with a physical examination. Other tests such as an ECG and blood tests are carried out to determine risk factors and rule out other likely grounds. Low blood sugar may cause comparable symptoms.

PREVALENCE

In 2010, approximately 17 million people had a stroke and 33 million people in the past had stroke and were still alive. Among 1990 and 2010, the numbers of strokes which occurred each year decreased by roughly 10% in the developed world and enlarged by 10% in the developing world. In 2013, stroke was the second most recurrent cause of death after coronary artery disease, accounting for 6.4 million deaths. About 3.3 million deaths resulted from ischemic stroke whereas 3.2 million deaths resulted due to hemorrhagic stroke. About half of people who have had a stroke live less than one year. In general, two thirds of strokes occurred in persons more than 65 years old.

Stroke is a major health problem in India. A recent community survey in the eastern Indian city of Kolkata reported the incidence rate of stroke to be 545/Lakh population. In a year usually 145/Lakh person's suffer the incidence of stroke. These rates, age standardised to world standard population, are similar to or higher than many Western nations. These rates are also much higher than those reported previously from other parts of India. Stroke burden in India has been growing in the last few decades, in distinction to developed countries, where stroke incidence has decrease.

The reasons for a rise in stroke burden in India include smoking, increasing durability of life, and change in lifestyle accompanying modernisation. As per as the case of India, average life expectancy raised from 41.2 years in 1951-1961 to 61.4 years in 1991-1996. Indians may also be genetically prone to stroke due to a high prevalence of the metabolic syndrome consisting of central obesity, high levels of triglycerides, and low levels of HDL cholesterol with or without glucose intolerance.

SIGNS AND SYMPTOMS OF STROKE

The signs and symptoms regularly emerge soon after the stroke incidence. If symptoms last less than one or two hours it is known as a transient ischemic attack. Hemorrhagic strokes may also be associated with a severe headache. The symptoms of a stroke can be permanent. Long term complication may comprise pneumonia or loss of bladder control.

- Sudden numbness or weakness in the face, arm, or leg, especially on one side of the body.
- Unexpected confusion, trouble in speaking, or difficulty in understanding speech.
- Sudden difficulty to see by one or both eyes.

- Sudden problem in walking, dizziness, loss of balance, or lack of co-ordination.
- Sudden severe headache with unknown cause.

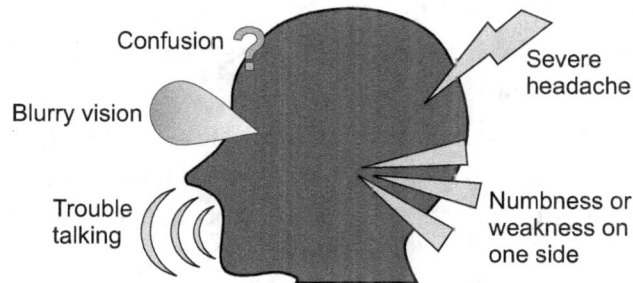

Fig. 13.2: Symptoms of Stroke

CAUSES

A stroke occurs when the blood supply to your brain is interrupted or reduced. This deprives your brain of oxygen and nutrients, which can cause your brain cells to die. The blocked artery (ischemic stroke), leaking or bursting of blood vessel (hemorrhagic stroke) leads to stroke. Some people may experience only a temporary disruption of blood flow to their brain transient ischemic attack [TIA] (Fig. 13.3).

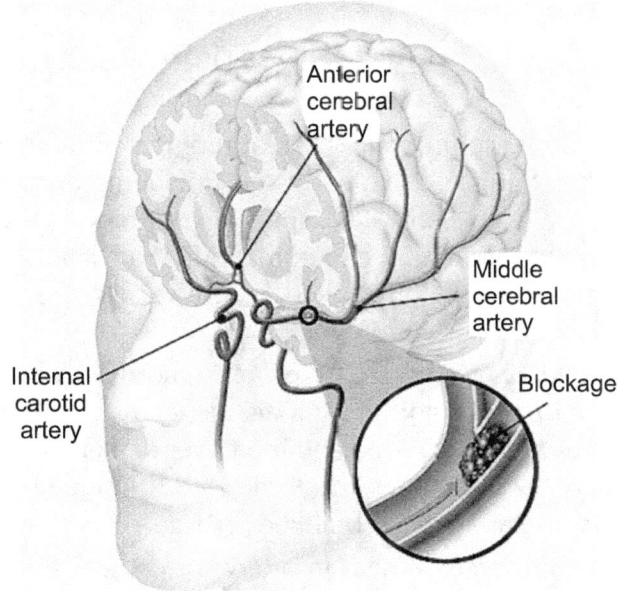

Fig. 13.3: Transient ischemic attack

(1) Ischemic Stroke

About 85% of strokes are ischemic strokes. Ischemic strokes occur when the arteries of brain become narrowed or blocked, causing severely decreased blood flow (ischemia).

Most the regular ischemic strokes include:

a. **Thrombotic stroke:** These occurs when a blood clot (thrombus) forms in one of the arteries which supply blood to brain. A clot can be caused due to fatty deposits i.e. plaque that build up in arteries and cause reduced blood flow (atherosclerosis) or other arterial environment.

b. **Embolic stroke:** This occurs when a blood clot or other debris forms away from your brain. Commonly in our heart is sweep through bloodstream to lodge in narrower brain arteries. Such type of blood clot is called an embolus.

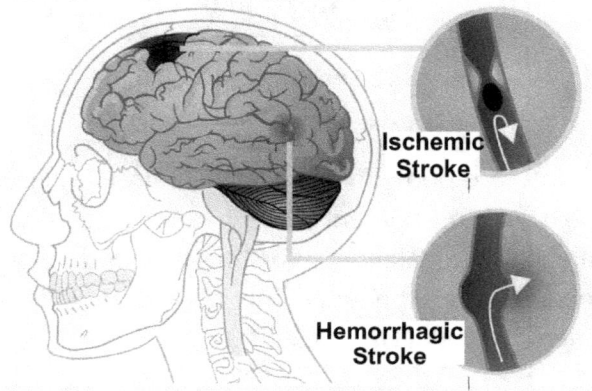

Fig. 13.4: Types of stroke

(2) Hemorrhagic Stroke

It occurs when a blood vessel in brain leaks or ruptures. Brain hemorrhages can result from lots of circumstances that affect blood vessels, including uncontrolled hypertension, over treatment with anticoagulants and weak spots in your blood vessel walls (aneurysms). A rare cause of hemorrhage is arteriovenous malformation it is a condition where the rupture of an abnormal tangle of thin-walled blood vessels present at birth. Types of hemorrhagic stroke includes:

i. **Intracerebral hemorrhage:** In such type of hemorrhage, a blood vessel of brain burst and spill into surrounding brain tissue, damaging brain cells. Brain cells beyond leak are rundown of blood and moreover damaged. A high blood pressure, trauma, vascular malformations, use of blood thinning medicine and other conditions may cause an intracerebral hemorrhage.

ii. **Subarachnoid hemorrhage:** When an artery on or near the plane of brain bursts and spills into the space between the surface of brain and skull it is called as subarachnoid hemorrhage. Such kind of bleeding is usually signaled by a sudden, severe headache. It is commonly caused due to bursting of a small sack-shaped or berry-shaped out pouching on an artery known as an aneurysm. After hemorrhage, the blood vessels in brain may widen and narrow randomly (vasospasm), causing brain cell damage by further limiting blood flow.

COMMON MYTHS AND MISUNDERSTANDINGS

Strokes are rare.

The World Health Organisation estimated that in 1990, out of 9.4 million deaths in India, 619,000 deaths were due to stroke, giving a mortality rate of 73 per 100,000 populations. In the same year, the number of deaths caused by stroke were 22 times that due to malaria, 1.4 times that due to tuberculos s, four times that due to rheumatic heart disease and almost equal to that due to ischemic heart disease. A little fights back physically, with difficulties in walking, chatting or dressing themselves. Others cope with cognitive challenges in reading, learning, remembering or planning.

Strokes can not be prevented.

In many cases, stroke can be prohibited by healthy choices. As with any cardiovascular disease, you can lower your risk by eating a healthy diet, exercising, not smoking, moderate alcohol and maintenance of a healthy body weight. Take the Heart and Stroke Risk Assessment to get started on a healthier lifestyle today.

Only older people have strokes.

Strokes are more general in elder people, (following age 55, the risk doubles each 10 years), but they can hit at any times even in infancy.

If someone has a stroke, you should drive them to hospital.

With stroke, fast reply is vital. If clot-busting drugs are administer within a few hours of the onset of symptoms, the chances for recovery are much higher. If you think you or someone you know is having a stroke, call emergency health services immediately. Ambulances give the best access to medical care since paramedics can convey information to a hospital en-route, allowing treatment to start sooner.

All strokes are the same.

Strokes are similar to fingerprints, no two are the same. Several strokes take place when the flow of blood to the brain is episodic, whereas others are caused by the rupture of blood vessels into the brain. How fit a patient recover largely depends on the kind of stroke and on how much of their brain was hurt, which parts were affected and the state of their health prior to the stroke.

Life is after stroke.

There is life subsequent to stroke. Approximately, all survivors improve to some extent. With good rehabilitation and support, many who survive a stroke can regain their independence and confidence.

MANAGEMENT

The 80% of all strokes are avoidable. It starts with managing key risk factors, counting high blood pressure, cigarette smoking, atrial fibrillation and physical inactivity. Over half of all strokes caused due to uncontrolled hypertension or high blood pressure, making it the most important risk factor to control.

Medical treatments may be used to control high blood pressure or deal with atrial fibrillation in the middle of high-risk patients. These medicines includes:

Anticoagulants/Antiplatelets: Antiplatelet agents (aspirin) and anticoagulants (warfarin), interfere with the blood's capacity to clot and can play an important role in preventing stroke. Read more about anticoagulants.

Antihypertensives: These are medications which treat high blood pressure. Depends on the type of medication, it can lower blood pressure by opening the blood vessels, decreasing blood volume or decreasing the rate and force of heart contraction. Additionally, when arteries show plaque build-up or blockage, few medical procedures are warranted like:

(a) Carotid endarterectomy: It is also known as carotid artery surgery and is a procedure in which blood vessel blockage i.e. fatty plaque is surgically removed from carotid artery.

(b) Angioplasty/Stents: Sometimes doctors make use balloon angioplasty or implantable steel screens known as *stents* to treat cardiovascular disease and help to open up the blocked blood vessel.

IMPORTANCE OF LIFESTYLE

A person does not need to depend on medication alone to control your blood pressure. The number of lifestyle alterations that we can make, helps to lower blood pressure and the risk of stroke. Few people with mild hypertension are able to control blood pressure simply by choosing a healthy lifestyle.

Lifestyle changes not only lower blood pressure, but also increases the efficiency of blood pressure medication and reduce the risk of stroke, heart attack and diabetes. It is important to keep blood pressure down. Remember, the lower your blood pressure, the lower your risk of stroke. It is important that doctor confirms blood pressure measurement and way to know that is to get it checked regularly.

Keep Weight within a Healthy Range: Being overweight can increase blood pressure. It may also raise cholesterol and increase the risk of emergent diabetes. Set small down-to-earth goals for weight loss. There are no 'quick fixes' a sensible weight plan includes eating healthy foods and exercising regularly.

Eat Foods that are Good: It may also raise your cholesterol and increase the risk of developing diabetes.

- Leave the car at home for short trips or walk.
- Get off the bus or train stop early to move some leg.
- Catch up the stairs case instead of the lift for routine in building.
- Wash the car yourself or get out in the garden.
- Play with the kids after school.
- Take up activities such as golf, tennis or cycling.

Cut down Alcohol: Stay within recommended limits for drinking alcohol. These are two standard drinks per day if you are male and one standard drink per day if you are female.

DO'S AND DONT'S IN STROKE

Do's

- Get your blood pressure checked before taking birth control pills.
- Talk to your doctor about medication if you are pregnant and have reasonably high blood pressure.
- Exercise regularly.
- If you are over 75, get screened for atrial fibrillation, the most common type of irregular heart rhythm.
- Have a complete diet filled of vegetables, grains, nuts, fruits, olive oil and foods low in saturated fats.

Don't

- Don't smoke, especially if you get migraine headaches with aura.
- Don't eat high-salt foods.
- Don't drink too much alcohol.

BIBLIOGRAPHY

- Aho K, Heliovaara M, Maatela J, Tuomi T, Palosuo T. Rheumatoid factors antedating clinical rheumatoid arthritis. J Rheumatol 1991; 18:1282–4.

- Alonso-Coello P, Mills E, Heels-Ansdell D, López-Yarto M, Zhou Q, Johanson JF, Guyatt G. Fibre for the treatment of hemorrhoids complications: a systematic review and meta-analysis. Am J Gastroenterol. 2006; 101:181–188.

- American Diabetes Association. Standards of medical care in diabetes-2010. Diabetes Care. 2010; 33(suppl 1):S11–61.

- Amin U, Khan N, Ali Bhat I. Prevalence and causes of infertility among women of Jammu and Kashmir. Int J Dev Res. 2015; 5:3771–3774.

- Barnard RJ, Jung T, Inkeles SB. Diet and exercise in the treatment of NIDDM: The need for early emphasis. Diabetes Care. 1994; 17:1–4.

- Brown B.W., Brauner C., Minnotte M.C. Non-cancer deaths in white adult cancer patients. J. Natl. Cancer Inst. 1993; 85:979–987.

- Caraci F., Copani A., Nicoletti F. and Drago F. (2010) Depression and Alzheimer's disease: neurobiological links and common pharmacological targets. Eur. J. Pharmacol. 626, 64–71.

- Carver J.R., Shapiro C.L., Ng A., Jacobs L., Schwartz C., Virgo K.S., Hagerty K.L., Somerfield M.R., Vaughn D.J., Panel A.C.S.E. American society of clinical oncology clinical evidence review on the ongoing care of adult cancer survivors: Cardiac and pulmonary late effects. J. Clin. Oncol. 2007; 25:3991–4008.

- Catrina AI, Deane KD, Scher JU. Gene, environment, microbiome and mucosal immune tolerance in rheumatoid arthritis. Rheumatology 2014; Advance Access published 23 December 2014, doi: 10.1093/rheumatology/keu469.

- Catrina AI, Ytterberg AJ, Reynisdottir G, Malmstrom V, Klareskog L. Lungs, joints and immunity against citrullinated proteins in rheumatoid arthritis. Nat Rev Rheumatol 2014; 10:645–53.

- Chapman J.A., Meng D., Shepherd L., Parulekar W., Ingle J.N., Muss H.B., Palmer M., Yu C., Goss P.E. Competing causes of death from a randomized trial of extended adjuvant endocrine therapy for breast cancer. J. Natl. Cancer Inst. 2008; 100:252–260.

- Chen D.-C., Chung Y.-F., Yeh Y.-T., Chaung H.-C., Kuo F.-C., Fu O.-Y., Chen H.-Y., Hou M.-F., Yuan S.-S.F. Serum adiponectin and leptin levels in Taiwanese breast cancer patients. Cancer Lett.2006; 237:109–114.

- Chlebowski R.T., Aiello E., McTiernan A. Weight loss in breast cancer patient management. J. Clin. Oncol. 2002; 20:1128–1143.

- Chow CK, Jolly S, Rao-Melacini P, Fox KA, Anand SS, Yusuf S. Association of diet, exercise, and smoking modification with risk of early cardiovascular events after acute coronary syndromes. Circulation. 2010; 121(6):750-758.

- Chung YC, Hou YC, Pan AC. Endoglin (CD105) expression in the development of haemorrhoids. Eur J Clin Invest. 2004; 34:107–112.

- Clinical Practice Committee, American Gastroenterological Association. American Gastroenterological Association medical position statement: Diagnosis and treatment of hemorrhoids. Gastroenterology. 2004; 126:1461–1462.

- Csernansky J. G., Dong H., Fagan A. M., Wang L., Xiong C., Holtzman D. M. and Morris J. C. (2006) Plasma cortisol and progression of dementia in subjects with Alzheimer type dementia. Am. J. Psychiatry 163, 2164–2169.

- Cuadrado-Tejedor M., Ricobaraza A., Frechilla D., Franco R., Pérez-Mediavilla A. and Garcia-Osta A. (2012) Chronic mild stress accelerates the onset and progression of the Alzheimer's disease phenotype in Tg2576 mice. J. Alzheimer's Dis. 28, 567–578.

- Fontaine KR, Cheskin LJ, Barofsky I. Health related quality of life in obese persons seeking treatment. J Fam Pract. 1996; 43:265–279.

- Gaur DS, Talekar MS, Pathak V. Alcohol intake and cigarette smoking: impact of two major lifestyle factors on male fertility. Indian J Pathol Microbiol. 2010; 53:35–40.

- Gudmundsdottir SL, Flanders WD, Augestad LB. Physical activity and fertility in women: the North-Trøndelag Health Study. Hum Reprod. 2009; 24:3196–3204.

- Homan GF, Davies M, Norman R. The impact of lifestyle factors on reproductive performance in the general population and those undergoing infertility treatment: a review. Hum Reprod Update. 2007; 13:209–223.

- Kamali Fard M, Alizadeh R, Sehati F, Golzadeh M. The effect of lifestyle on the rate of preterm rate. J Ardabil Univ Med Sci. 2007; 10:55–63.

- Karlson EW, van Schaardenburg D, van der Helm-van Mil AH. Strategies to predict rheumatoid arthritis development in at risk populations. Rheumatology 2014; Advance Access published 4 August 2014, doi: 10.1093/rheumatology/keu287.

- Kushi L.H., Doyle C., McCullough M., Rock C.L., Demark-Wahnefried W., Bandera E.V., Gapstur S., Patel A.V., Andrews K., Gansler T. American cancer society guidelines on nutrition and physical activity for cancer prevention: Reducing the risk of cancer with healthy food choices and physical activity. CA: Cancer J. Clin. 2012; 62:30–67.

- Lammich S., Kojro E., Postina R., Gilbert S., Pfeiffer R., Jasionowski M., Haass C. and Fahrenholz F. (1999) Constitutive and regulated alpha-secretase cleavage of Alzheimer's amyloid precursor protein by a disintegrin metalloprotease. Proc. Natl Acad. Sc. USA 96, 3922–3927.

- Liao D, Cooper L, Toole J. The prevalence and severity of white lesions, their relationship with age, ethnicity, gender and cardiovascular disease risk factors: ARIC Study. Neuroepidemiology. 1997; 16(3):149–162.

- Loder PB, Kamm MA, Nicholls RJ, Phillips RK. Haemorrhoids: pathology, pathophysiology and aetiology. Br J Surg. 1994; 81:946–954.

- Lohsiriwat V. Approach to hemorrhoids. Curr Gastroenterol Rep. 2013; 15:332.

- Lohsiriwat V. Hemorrhoids: from basic pathophysiology to clinical management. World J Gastroenterol. 2012; 18:2009–2017.

- Marcello E., Epis R., Saraceno C. and Di Luca M. (2012) Synaptic dysfunction in Alzheimer's disease. Adv Exp Med Biol. 970, 573–601.

- Morgado PJ, Suárez JA, Gómez LG, Morgado PJ. Histoclinical basis for a new classification of hemorrhoidal disease. Dis Colon Rectum. 1988; 31:474–480.

- Nalivaeva N. N., Belyaev N. D., Kerridge C. and Turner A. J. (2014) Amyloid clearing proteins and their epigenetic regulation as a therapeutic target in Alzheimer's disease. Front. Aging Neurosci. 6, 235.

- Panagiotakos DB, Pitsavos C, Chrysohoou C, Stefanadis C. The epidemiology of Type 2 diabetes mellitus in Greek adults: The ATTICA study. Diabet Med. 2005; 22:1581–8.
- Pedersen M, Stripp C, Klarlund M, et al. Diet and risk of rheumatoid arthritis in a prospective cohort. J Rheumatol 2005; 32:1249–52.
- Pekmezi D.W., Demark-Wahnefried W. Updated evidence in support of diet and exercise interventions in cancer survivors. Acta Oncol. 2011; 50:167–178.
- Pigot F, Siproudhis L, Allaert FA. Risk factors associated with hemorrhoidal symptoms in specialized consultation. Gastroenterol Clin Biol. 2005; 29:1270–1274.
- Pi-Sunyer FX. Health implication on obesity. Am J Clin Nutr. 1991; 53(6):1595s–1603s.
- Ramzisham AR, Sagap I, Nadeson S, Ali IM, Hasni MJ. Prospective randomized clinical trial on suction elastic band ligator versus forceps ligator in the treatment of haemorrhoids. Asian J Surg. 2005; 28:241–245.
- Report of the WHO consultation on obesity. Geneva: WHO; 1998. Prevention and Management of the Global Epidemic of Obesity.
- Sanchez-Tainta A, Estruch R, Bullo M, Corella D, Gomez-Gracia E, Fiol M. Adherence to a Mediterranean-type diet and reduced prevalence of clustered cardiovascular risk factors in a cohort of 3,204 high-risk patients. Eur J Cardiovasc Prev Rehabil. 2008; 15:589–93.
- Schroder H. Protective mechanisms of the Mediterranean diet in obesity and type 2 diabetes. J Nutr Biochem. 2007; 18:149–60.
- Sidney S, Rosamond WD, Howard VJ, Luepker RV. The "Heart Disease and Stroke Statistics, 2013 Update" and the Need for a National Cardiovascular Surveillance System. Circulation. 2013; 127(1):21–23.
- Sogaard M., Thomsen R.W., Bossen K.S., Sorensen H.T., Norgaard M. The impact of comorbidity on cancer survival: A review. Clin. Epidemiol. 2013; 5:3–29.
- Thomson WH. The nature and cause of haemorrhoids. Proc R Soc Med. 1975; 68:574–575.
- Tucker H, George E, Barnett D, Longson C. NICE Technology Appraisal on Stapled Haemorrhoidopexy for the Treatment of Haemorrhoids. Ann R Coll Surg Engl. 2008; 90:82–84.
- Van Erning F.N., van Steenbergen L.N., Lemmens V.E., Rutten H.J., Martijn H., van Spronsen D.J., Janssen-Heijnen M.L. Conditional survival for long-term colorectal cancer survivors in the Netherlands: Who do best? Eur. J. Cancer. 2014; 50:1731–1739.
- Wilson R. S., Arnold S. E., Schneider J. A., Kelly J. F., Tang Y. and Bennett D. A. (2006) Chronic psychological distress and risk of Alzheimer's disease in old age. Neuroepidemiology 27, 143–153.
- World Health Organization. Obesity: Preventing and Managing the Global Epidemic. Geneva: Report of a WHO consultation on obesity; 1998.
- Yeung TM, D'Souza ND. Quality analysis of patient information on surgical treatment of haemorrhoids on the internet. Ann R Coll Surg Engl. 2013; 95:341–344.

Index

www.ingramcontent.com/pod-product-compliance
Lightning Source LLC
Chambersburg PA
CBHW080824020726
47501CB00009B/2416